PARKER PYNE INVESTIGATES

AGATHA CHRISTIE is known throughout the world as the Queen of Crime. Her seventy-seven detective novels and books of stories have been translated into every major language, and her sales are calculated in tens of millions.

She began writing at the end of the First World War, when she created Hercule Poirot, the little Belgian detective with the egg-shaped head and the passion for order – the most popular sleuth in fiction since Sherlock Holmes. Poirot, Miss Marple and her other detectives have appeared in films, radio programmes and stage plays based on her books.

Agatha Christie also wrote six romantic novels under the pseudonym Mary Wastmacott, several plays and a book of poems; as well, she assisted her archaeologist husband Sir Max Mallowan on many expeditions to the Near East.

She died in 1976.

Available in Fontana by the same author

Dead Man's Folly
A Pocket Full of Rye
Appointment With Death
Towards Zero
Hickory Dickory Dock
Five Little Pigs
After the Funeral
By the Pricking of My Thumbs
Ten Little Niggers
The Listerdale Mystery
Postern of Fate
4.50 from Paddington
Miss Marple's Final Cases
Murder on the Orient Express
N or M?
Sparkling Cyanide
Cards on the Table
The Thirteen Problems
They Do It With Mirrors
The Murder at the Vicarage

and many others

AGATHA CHRISTIE

Parker Pyne Investigates

FONTANA / Collins

First published by William Collins Sons & Co. Ltd 1934
First issued in Fontana Paperbacks 1962
Tenth Impression February 1982

Made and printed in Great Britain by
William Collins Sons & Co. Ltd, Glasgow

CONTENTS

THE CASE OF THE MIDDLE-AGED WIFE

Four grunts, an indignant voice asking why nobody could leave a hat alone, a slammed door, and Mr. Packington had departed to catch the eight-forty-five to the city. Mrs. Packington sat on at the breakfast table. Her face was flushed, her lips were pursed, and the only reason she was not crying was that at the last minute anger had taken the place of grief. "I won't stand it," said Mrs. Packington. "I won't stand it!" She remained for some moments brooding, and then murmured: "The minx. Nasty sly little cat! How George can be such a fool!"

Anger faded; grief came back. Tears came into Mrs. Packington's eyes and rolled slowly down her middle-aged cheeks. "It's all very well to say I won't stand it, but what can I do?"

Suddenly she felt alone, helpless, utterly forlorn. Slowly she took up the morning paper and read, not for the first time, an advertisement on the front page.

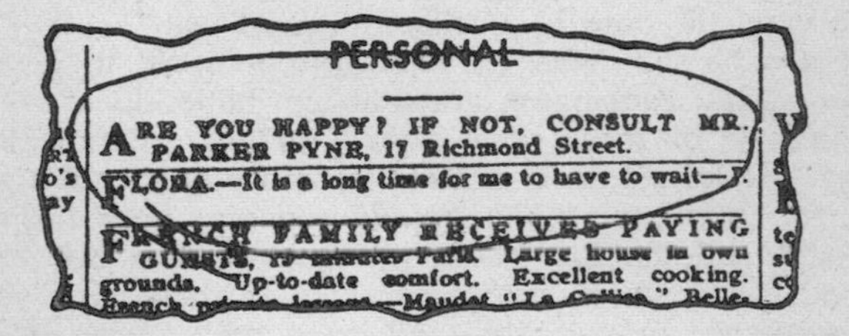

"Absurd!" said Mrs. Packington. "Utterly absurd." Then: "After all, I might just see . . ."

Which explains why at eleven o'clock Mrs. Packington, a little nervous, was being shown into Mr. Parker Pyne's private office.

As has been said, Mrs. Packington was nervous, but somehow or other, the mere sight of Mr. Parker Pyne brought a feeling of reassurance. He was large, not to say fat; he had a bald head of noble proportions, strong glasses, and little twinkling eyes.

"Pray sit down," said Mr. Parker Pyne. "You have come in answer to my advertisement?" he added helpfully.

"Yes," said Mrs. Packington, and stopped there.

"And you are not happy," said Mr. Parker Pyne in a cheerful, matter-of-fact voice. "Very few people are. You would really be surprised if you knew how few people are happy."

"Indeed?" said Mrs. Packington, not feeling, however, that it mattered whether other people were unhappy or not.

"Not interesting to you, I know," said Mr. Parker Pyne, "but very interesting to *me*. You see, for thirty-five years of my life I have been engaged in the compiling of statistics in a government office. Now I have retired, and it has occurred to me to use the experience I have gained in a novel fashion. It is all so simple. Unhappiness can be classified under five main heads—no more, I assure you. Once you know the cause of a malady, the remedy should not be impossible.

"I stand in the place of the doctor. The doctor first diagnoses the patient's disorder, then he proceeds to recommend a course of treatment. There are cases where no treatment can be of any avail. If that is so, I say frankly that I can do nothing. But I assure you, Mrs. Packington, that if I undertake a case, the cure is practically guaranteed."

Could it be so? Was this nonsense, or could it, perhaps, be true? Mrs. Packington gazed at him hopefully.

"Shall we diagnose your case?" said Mr. Parker Pyne, smiling. He leaned back in his chair and brought the tips of his fingers together. "The trouble concerns your husband. You have had, on the whole, a happy married life. Your husband has, I think, prospered. I think there is a young lady concerned in the case—perhaps a young lady in your husband's office."

"A typist," said Mrs. Packington. "A nasty made-up little minx, all lipstick and silk stockings and curls." The words rushed from her.

Mr. Parker Pyne nodded in a soothing manner. "There is no real harm in it—that is your husband's phrase, I have no doubt."

"His very words."

"Why, therefore, should he not enjoy a pure friendship with this young lady, and be able to bring a little brightness, a little pleasure, into her dull existence? Poor child, she has so little fun. Those, I imagine, are his sentiments."

Mrs. Packington nodded with vigour. "Humbug—all humbug! He takes her on the river—I'm fond of going on the river myself, but five or six years ago he said it interfered with his golf. But he can give up golf for *her*. I like the theatre—George has always said he's too tired to go out at night. Now he takes her out to dance—*dance*! And comes back at three in the morning. I—I——"

"And doubtless he deplores the fact that women are so jealous, so unreasonably jealous when there is absolutely no cause for jealousy?"

Again Mrs. Packington nodded. "That's it." She asked sharply: "How do you know all this?"

"Statistics," Mr. Parker Pyne said simply.

"I'm so miserable," said Mrs. Packington. "I've always been a good wife to George. I worked my fingers to the bone in our early days. I helped him to get on. I've never looked at any other man. His things are always mended, he gets good meals, and the house is well and economically run. And now that we've got on in the world and could enjoy ourselves and go about a bit and do all the things I've looked forward to doing some day—well, this!" She swallowed hard.

Mr. Parker Pyne nodded gravely. "I assure you I understand your case perfectly."

"And—can you do anything?" She asked it almost in whisper.

"Certainly, my dear lady. There is a cure. Oh yes, there is a cure."

"What is it?" She waited, round-eyed and expectant.

Mr. Parker Pyne spoke quietly and firmly. "You will place yourself in my hands, and the fee will be two hundred guineas."

"Two hundred guineas!"

"Exactly. You can afford to pay such a fee, Mrs. Packington. You would pay that sum for an operation. Happiness is just as important as bodily health."

"I pay you afterwards, I suppose?"

"On the contrary," said Mr. Parker Pyne. "You pay me in advance."

Mrs. Packington rose. "I'm afraid I don't see my way ——"

"To buying a pig in a poke?" said Mr. Parker Pyne cheerfully. "Well, perhaps you're right. It's a lot of money to risk. You've got to trust me, you see. You've got to pay the money and take a chance. Those are my terms."

"Two hundred guineas!"

"Exactly. Two hundred guineas. It's a lot of money. Good-morning, Mrs. Packington. Let me know if you change your mind." He shook hands with her, smiling in an unperturbed fashion.

When she had gone he pressed a buzzer on his desk. A forbidding-looking young woman with spectacles answered it.

"A file, please, Miss Lemon. And you might tell Claude that I am likely to want him shortly."

"A new client?"

"A new client. At the moment she has jibbed, but she will come back. Probably this afternoon about four. Enter her."

"Schedule A?"

"Schedule A, of course. Interesting how everyone thinks his own case unique. Well, well, warn Claude. Not too exotic, tell him. No scent and he'd better get his hair cut short."

It was a quarter-past four when Mrs. Packington once more entered Mr. Parker Pyne's office. She drew out a cheque book, made out a cheque and passed it to him. A receipt was given.

"And now?" Mrs. Packington looked at him hopefully.

"And now," said Mr. Parker Pyne, smiling, "you will return home. By the first post to-morrow you will receive certain instructions which I shall be glad if you will carry out."

Mrs. Packington went home in a state of pleasant anticipation. Mr. Packington came home in a defensive mood, ready to argue his position if the scene at the breakfast table was reopened. He was relieved, however, to find that his wife did not seem to be in a combative mood. She was unusually thoughtful.

George listened to the radio and wondered whether that dear child Nancy would allow him to give her a fur coat. She was very proud, he knew. He didn't want to offend her. Still, she had complained of the cold. That tweed coat of hers was a cheap affair; it didn't keep the cold out. He could put it so that she wouldn't mind, perhaps . . .

They must have another evening out soon. It was a pleasure to take a girl like that to a smart restaurant. He could see several young fellows were envying him. She was uncommonly pretty. And she liked him. To her, as she had told him, he didn't seem a bit old.

He looked up and caught his wife's eye. He felt suddenly guilty, which annoyed him. What a narrow-minded, suspicious woman Maria was! She grudged him any little bit of happiness.

He switched off the radio and went to bed.

Mrs. Packington received two unexpected letters the following morning. One was a printed form confirming an appointment at a noted beauty specialist's. The second was an appointment with a dressmaker. The third was from Mr. Parker Pyne, requesting the pleasure of her company at lunch at the Ritz that day.

Mr. Packington mentioned that he might not be home to dinner that evening as he had to see a man on business. Mrs. Packington merely nodded absently, and Mr. Packington left the house congratulating himself on having escaped the storm.

The beauty specialist was impressive. Such neglect! Madame, but *why*? This should have been taken in hand years ago. However, it was not too late.

Things were done to her face; it was pressed and kneaded and steamed. It had mud applied to it. It had creams applied to it. It was dusted with powder. There were various finishing touches.

At last she was given a mirror. "I believe I *do* look younger," she thought to herself.

The dressmaking seance was equally exciting. She emerged feeling smart, modish, up-to-date.

At half-past one, Mrs. Packington kept her appointment at the Ritz. Mr. Parker Pyne, faultlessly dressed and carrying with him his atmosphere of soothing reassurance, was waiting for her.

"Charming," he said, an experienced eye sweeping her from head to foot. "I have ventured to order you a White Lady."

Mrs. Packington, who had not contracted the cocktail habit, made no demur. As she sipped the exciting fluid gingerly, she listened to her benevolent instructor.

"Your husband, Mrs. Packington," said Mr. Parker Pyne, "must be made to Sit Up. You understand—to Sit Up. To assist in that, I am going to introduce to you a young friend of mine. You will lunch with him to-day."

At that moment a young man came along, looking from side to side. He espied Mr. Parker Pyne and came gracefully towards them.

"Mr. Claude Luttrell, Mrs. Packington."

Mr. Claude Luttrell was perhaps just short of thirty. He was graceful, debonair, perfectly dressed, extremely handsome.

"Delighted to meet you," he murmured.

Three minutes later Mrs. Packington was facing her new mentor at a small table for two.

She was shy at first, but Mr. Luttrell soon put her at her ease. He knew Paris well and had spent a good deal of time on the Riviera. He asked Mrs. Packington if she were fond of dancing. Mrs. Packington said she was, but that she seldom got any dancing nowadays as Mr. Packington didn't care to go out in the evenings.

"But he couldn't be so unkind as to keep *you* at home," said Claude Luttrell, smiling and displaying a dazzling row of teeth. "Women will not tolerate male jealousy in these days."

Mrs. Packington nearly said that jealousy didn't enter into the question. But the words remained unspoken. After all, it was an agreeable idea.

Claude Luttrell spoke airily of night clubs. It was settled that on the following evening Mrs. Packington and Mr. Luttrell should patronise the popular Lesser Archangel.

Mrs. Packington was a little nervous about announcing this fact to her husband. George, she felt, would think it extraordinary and possibly ridiculous. But she was saved all trouble on this score. She had been too nervous to make her announcement at breakfast, and at two o'clock a telephone message came to the effect that Mr. Packington would be dining in town.

The evening was a great success. Mrs. Packington had been a good dancer as a girl and under Claude Luttrell's skilled guidance she soon picked up modern steps. He congratulated her on her gown and also on the arrangement of her hair. (An appointment had been made for her that morning with a fashionable hairdresser.) On bidding her farewell, he kissed her hand in a most thrilling manner. Mrs. Packington had not enjoyed an evening so much for years.

A bewildering ten days ensued. Mrs. Packington lunched, teaed, tangoed, dined, danced and supped. She heard all about Claude Luttrell's sad childhood. She heard the sad circumstances in which his father lost all his money. She heard of his tragic romance and his embittered feelings towards women generally.

On the eleventh day they were dancing at the Red Admiral. Mrs. Packington saw her spouse before he saw her. George was with the young lady from his office. Both couples were dancing.

"Hallo, George," said Mrs. Packington lightly, as their orbits brought them together.

It was with considerable amusement that she saw her husband's face grow first red, then purple with astonishment. With the astonishment was blended an expression of guilt detected.

Mrs. Packington felt amusedly mistress of the situation. Poor old George! Seated once more at her table, she watched them. How stout he was, how bald, how terribly he bounced on his feet! He danced in the style of twenty years ago. Poor George, how terribly he wanted to be young! And that poor girl he was dancing with had to pretend to like it. She looked bored enough now, her face over his shoulder where he couldn't see it.

How much more enviable, thought Mrs. Packington contentedly, was her own situation. She glanced at the perfect Claude, now tactfully silent. How well he understood her. He never jarred—as husbands so inevitably did jar after a lapse of years.

She looked at him again. Their eyes met. He smiled; his beautiful dark eyes, so melancholy, so romantic, looked tenderly into hers.

"Shall we dance again?" he murmured.

They danced again. It was heaven!

She was conscious of George's apologetic gaze following them. It had been the idea, she remembered, to make George jealous. What a long time ago that was! She really didn't want George to be jealous now. It might upset him. Why should he be upset, poor thing? Everyone was so happy. . . .

Mr. Packington had been home an hour when Mrs. Packington got in. He looked bewildered and unsure of himself.

"Humph," he remarked. "So you're back."

Mrs. Packington cast off an evening wrap which had cost her forty guineas that very morning. "Yes," she said, smiling. "I'm back."

George coughed. "Er—rather odd meeting you."

"Wasn't it?" said Mrs. Packington.

"I—well, I thought it would be a kindness to take that girl somewhere. She's been having a lot of trouble at home. I thought—well, kindness, you know."

Mrs. Packington nodded. Poor old George—bouncing on his feet and getting so hot and being so pleased with himself.

"Who's that chap you were with? I don't know him, do I?"

"Luttrell, his name is. Claude Luttrell."

"How did you come across him?"

"Oh, someone introduced me," said Mrs. Packington vaguely.

"Rather a queer thing for you to go out dancing—at your time of life. Mustn't make a fool of yourself, my dear."

Mrs. Packington smiled. She was feeling much too kindly to the universe in general to make the obvious reply. "A change is always nice," she said amiably.

"You've got to be careful, you know. A lot of these lounge-lizard fellows going about. Middle-aged women sometimes make awful fools of themselves. I'm just warning you, my dear. I don't like to see you doing anything unsuitable."

"I find the exercise very beneficial," said Mrs. Packington.

"Um—yes."

"I expect you do, too," said Mrs. Packington kindly. "The great thing is to be happy, isn't it? I remember your saying so one morning at breakfast, about ten days ago."

Her husband looked at her sharply, but her expression was devoid of sarcasm. She yawned.

"I must go to bed. By the way, George, I've been dreadfully extravagant lately. Some terrible bills will be coming in. You don't mind, do you?"

"Bills?" said Mr. Packington.

"Yes. For clothes. And massage. And hair treatment. Wickedly extravagant I've been—but I know you don't mind."

She passed up the stairs. Mr. Packington remained with his mouth open. Maria had been amazingly nice about this evening's business; she hadn't seemed to care at all. But it was a pity she had suddenly taken to spending Money. Maria—that model of economy!

Women! George Packington shook his head. The scrapes that girl's brothers had been getting into lately. Well, he'd been glad to help. All the same—and dash it all, things weren't going too well in the city.

Sighing, Mr. Packington in his turn slowly climbed the stairs.

Sometimes words that fail to make their effect at the time are remembered later. Not till the following morning did certain words uttered by Mr. Packington really penetrate his wife's consciousness.

Lounge lizards; middle-aged women; awful fools of themselves.

Mrs. Packington was courageous at heart. She sat down and faced facts. A gigolo. She had read all about gigolos in the papers. Had read, too, of the follies of middle-aged women.

Was Claude a gigolo? She supposed he was. But then, gigolos were paid for and Claude always paid for her. Yes, but it was Mr. Parker Pyne who paid, not Claude—or, rather, it was really her own two hundred guineas.

Was she a middle-aged fool? Did Claude Luttrell laugh at her behind her back? Her face flushed at the thought.

Well, what of it? Claude was a gigolo. She was a middle-aged fool. She supposed she should have given him something. A gold cigarette case. That sort of thing.

A queer impulse drove her out there and then to Asprey's. The cigarette case was chosen and paid for. She was to meet Claude at Claridge's for lunch.

As they were sipping coffee she produced it from her bag. "A little present," she murmured.

He looked up, frowned. "For me?"

"Yes. I—I hope you like it."

His hand closed over it and he slid it violently across the table. "Why do you give me that? I won't take it. Take it back. Take it back, I say." He was angry. His dark eyes flashed.

She murmured, "I'm sorry," and put it away in her bag again.

There was constraint between them that day.

The following morning he rang her up. "I must see you. Can I come to your house this afternoon?"

She told him to come at three o'clock.

He arrived very white, very tense. They greeted each other. The constraint was more evident.

Suddenly he sprang up and stood facing her. "What do you think I am? That is what I've come to ask you. We've been friends, haven't we? Yes, friends. But all the same, you think I'm—well, a gigolo. A creature who lives on women. A lounge lizard. You do, don't you?"

"No, no."

He swept aside her protest. His face had gone very white. "You *do* think that! Well, it's true. That's what I've come to say. It's true! I had my orders to take you about, to amuse you, to make love to you, to make you forget your husband. That was my job. A despicable one, eh?"

"Why are you telling me this?" she asked.

"Because I'm through with it. I can't carry on with it. Not with *you*. You're different. You're the kind of woman I could believe in, trust, adore. You think I'm just saying this; that it's part of the game." He came closer to her. "I'm going to prove to you it isn't. I'm going away—because of you. I'm going to make myself into a man instead of the loathsome creature I am because of you."

He took her suddenly in his arms. His lips closed on hers. Then he released her and stood away.

"Good-bye. I've been a rotter—always. But I swear it will be different now. Do you remember once saying you liked to read the advertisements in the Agony column? On this day every year you'll find there a message from me saying that I remember and am making good. You'll know, then, all you've meant to me. One thing more. I've taken nothing from you. I want you to take something from me." He drew a plain gold seal ring from his finger. "This was my mother's. I'd like you to have it. Now good-bye."

He left her standing there amazed, the gold ring in her hand.

George Packington came home early. He found his wife gazing into the fire with a faraway look. She spoke kindly but absently to him.

"Look here, Maria," he jerked out suddenly. "About that girl?"

"Yes, dear?"

"I—I never meant to upset you, you know. About her. Nothing in it."

"I know. I was foolish. See as much as you like of her if it makes you happy."

These words, surely, should have cheered George Packington. Strangely enough, they annoyed him. How could you enjoy taking a girl about when your wife fairly urged you on? Dash it all, it wasn't decent! All that feeling of being a gay dog, of being a strong man playing with fire, fizzled out and died an ignominious death. George Packington felt suddenly tired and a great deal poorer in pocket. The girl was a shrewd little piece.

"We might go away together somewhere for a bit if you like, Maria?" he suggested timidly.

"Oh, never mind about me. I'm quite happy."

"But I'd like to take you away. We might go to the Riviera."

Mrs. Packington smiled at him from a distance.

Poor old George. She was fond of him. He was such a pathetic old dear. There was no secret splendour in his life as there was in hers. She smiled more tenderly still.

"That would be lovely, my dear," she said.

Mr. Parker Pyne was speaking to Miss Lemon. "Entertainment account?"

"One hundred and two pounds, fourteen and sixpence," said Miss Lemon.

The door was pushed open and Claude Luttrell entered. He looked moody.

"Morning, Claude," said Mr. Parker Pyne. "Everything go off satisfactorily?"

"I suppose so."

"The ring? What name did you put in it, by the way?"

"Matilda," said Claude gloomily. "1899."

"Excellent. What wording for the advertisement?"

"'Making good. Still remember. Claude.'"

"Make a note of that, please, Miss Lemon. The Agony column. November third for—let me see, expenses a hundred and two pounds, fourteen and six. Yes, for ten years, I think. That leaves us a profit of ninety-two pounds, two and fourpence. Adequate. Quite adequate."

Miss Lemon departed.

"Look here," Claude burst out. "I don't like this. It's a rotten game."

"My dear boy!"

"A rotten game. That was a decent woman—a good sort. Telling her all those lies, filling her up with this sob-stuff, dash it all, it makes me sick!"

Mr. Parker Pyne adjusted his glasses and looked at Claude with a kind of scientific interest. "Dear me!" he said dryly. "I do not seem to remember that your conscience ever troubled you during your somewhat—ahem!—notorious career. Your affairs on the Riviera were particularly brazen, and your exploitation of Mrs. Hattie West, the Californian Cucumber King's wife, was especially notable for the callous mercenary instinct you displayed."

"Well, I'm beginning to feel different," grumbled Claude. "It isn't—nice, this game."

Mr. Parker Pyne spoke in the voice of a head master admonishing a favourite pupil. "You have, my dear Claude, performed a meritorious action. You have given an unhappy woman what every woman needs—a romance. A woman tears a passion to pieces and gets no good from it, but a romance can be laid up in lavender and looked at all through the long years to come. I know human nature, my boy, and I tell you that a woman can feed on such an incident for years." He coughed. "We have discharged our commission to Mrs. Packington very satisfactorily."

"Well," muttered Claude, "I don't like it." He left the room.

Mr. Parker Pyne took a new file from a drawer. He wrote: "Interesting vestiges of a conscience noticeable in hardened Lounge Lizard. Note: Study developments."

THE CASE OF THE DISCONTENTED SOLDIER

Major Wilbraham hesitated outside the door of Mr. Parker Pyne's office to read, not for the first time, the advertisement from the morning paper which had brought him there. It was simple enough:

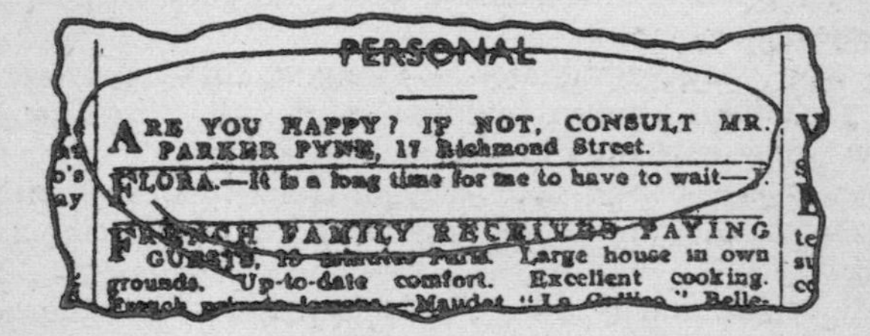

PERSONAL

ARE YOU HAPPY? IF NOT, CONSULT MR. PARKER PYNE, 17 Richmond Street.

FLORA.—It is a long time for me to have to wait—J.

FRENCH FAMILY RECEIVES PAYING GUESTS, [illegible] Park. Large house in own grounds. Up-to-date comfort. Excellent cooking. [illegible]

The major took a deep breath and abruptly plunged through the swing door leading to the outer office. A plain young woman looked up from her typewriter and glanced at him inquiringly.

"Mr. Parker Pyne?" said Major Wilbraham, blushing.

"Come this way, please."

He followed her into an inner office—into the presence of the bland Mr. Parker Pyne.

"Good-morning," said Mr. Pyne. "Sit down, won't you? And now tell me what I can do for you."

"My name is Wilbraham——" began the other.

"Major? Colonel?" said Mr. Pyne.

"Major."

"Ah! And recently returned from abroad? India? East Africa?"

"East Africa."

"A fine country, I believe. Well, so you are home again—and you don't like it. Is that the trouble?"

"You're absolutely right. Though how you knew——"

Mr. Parker Pyne waved an impressive hand. "It is my business to know. You see, for thirty-five years of my life I have been engaged in the compiling of statistics in a government office. Now I have retired and it has occurred to me to use the experience I have gained in a novel fashion. It is all so simple. Unhappiness can be classified under five main heads—no more I assure you. Once you know the cause of a malady, the remedy should not be impossible.

"I stand in the place of the doctor. The doctor first diagnoses the patient's disorder, then he recommends a course of treatment. There are cases where no treatment can be of any avail. If that is so, I say quite frankly that I can do nothing about it. But if I undertake a case, the cure is practically guaranteed.

"I can assure you, Major Wilbraham, that ninety-six per cent. of retired empire builders—as I call them—are unhappy. They exchange an active life, a life full of responsibility, a life of possible danger, for—what? Straitened means, a dismal climate and a general feeling of being a fish out of water."

"All you've said is true," said the major. "It's the boredom I object to. The boredom and the endless tittle-tattle about petty village matters. But what can I do about it? I've got a little money besides my pension. I've a nice cottage near Cobham. I can't afford to hunt or shoot or fish. I'm not married. My neighbours are all pleasant folk, but they've no ideas beyond this island."

"The long and short of the matter is that you find life tame," said Mr. Parker Pyne.

"Damned tame."

"You would like excitement, possibly danger?" asked Mr. Pyne.

The soldier shrugged. "There's no such thing in this tin-pot country."

"I beg your pardon," said Mr. Pyne seriously. "There you are wrong. There is plenty of danger, plenty of excitement, here in London if you know where to go for it. You have seen only the surface of our English life, calm, pleasant. But there is another side. If you wish it, I can show you that other side."

Major Wilbraham regarded him thoughtfully. There was something reassuring about Mr. Pyne. He was large, not to say fat; he had a bald head of noble proportions, strong glasses and little twinkling eyes. And he had an aura—an aura of dependability.

"I should warn you, however," continued Mr. Pyne, "that there is an element of risk."

The soldier's eye brightened. "That's all right," he said. Then, abruptly: "And—your fees?"

"My fee," said Mr. Pyne, "is fifty pounds, payable in advance. If in a month's time you are still in the same state of boredom, I will refund your money."

Wilbraham considered. "Fair enough," he said at last. "I agree. I'll give you a cheque now."

The transaction was completed. Mr. Parker Pyne pressed a buzzer on his desk.

"It is now one o'clock," he said. "I am going to ask you to take a young lady out to lunch." The door opened. "Ah, Madeleine, my dear, let me introduce Major Wilbraham, who is going to take you out to lunch."

Wilbraham blinked slightly, which was hardly to be wondered at. The girl who entered the room was dark, languorous, with wonderful eyes and long black lashes, a perfect complexion and a voluptuous scarlet mouth. Her exquisite clothes set off the swaying grace of her figure. From head to foot she was perfect.

"Er—delighted," said Major Wilbraham.

"Miss de Sara," said Mr. Parker Pyne.

"How very kind of you," murmured Madeleine de Sara.

"I have your address here," announced Mr. Parker Pyne. "To-morrow morning you will receive my further instructions."

Major Wilbraham and the lovely Madeleine departed.

It was three o'clock when Madeleine returned.

Mr. Parker Pyne looked up. "Well?" he demanded.

Madeleine shook her head. "Scared of me," she said. "Thinks I'm a vamp."

"I thought as much," said Mr. Parker Pyne. "You carried out my instructions?"

"Yes. We discussed the occupants of the other tables freely. The type he likes is fair-haired, blue-eyed, slightly anæmic, not too tall."

"That should be easy," said Mr. Pyne. "Get me Schedule B and let me see what we have in stock at present." He ran his finger down a list, finally stopping at a name. "Freda Clegg. Yes, I think Freda Clegg will do excellently. I had better see Mrs. Oliver about it."

The next day Major Wilbraham received a note, which read:

> On Monday morning next at eleven o'clock go to Eaglemont, Friars Lane, Hampstead, and ask for Mr. Jones. You will represent yourself as coming from the Guava Shipping Company.

Obediently on the following Monday (which happened to be Bank Holiday), Major Wilbraham set out for Eaglemont, Friars Lane. He set out, I say, but he never got there. For before he got there, something happened.

All the world and his wife seemed to be on their way to Hampstead. Major Wilbraham got entangled in crowds, suffocated in the tube and found it hard to discover the whereabouts of Friars Lane.

Friars Lane was a cul-de-sac, a neglected road full of ruts, with houses on either side standing back from the road. They were largish houses which had seen better days and had been allowed to fall into disrepair.

Wilbraham walked along peering at the half-erased names on the gate-posts, when suddenly he heard something that made him stiffen to attention. It was a kind of gurgling, half-choked cry.

It came again and this time it was faintly recognisable as the word "Help!" It came from inside the wall of the house he was passing.

Without a moment's hesitation, Major Wilbraham pushed open the rickety gate and sprinted noiselessly up the weed-covered drive. There in the shrubbery was a girl struggling in the grasp of two enormous Negroes. She was putting up a brave fight, twisting and turning and kicking. One Negro held his hand over her mouth in spite of her furious efforts to get her head free.

Intent on their struggle with the girl, neither of the blacks had noticed Wilbraham's approach. The first they knew of it was when a violent punch on the jaw sent the man who was covering the girl's mouth reeling backwards. Taken by surprise, the other man relinquished his hold of the girl and turned. Wilbraham was ready for him. Once again his fist shot out, and the Negro reeled backwards and fell. Wilbraham turned on the other man, who was closing in behind him.

But the two men had had enough. The second one rolled over, sat up; then, rising, he made a dash for the gate. His companion followed suit. Wilbraham started after them, but changed his mind and turned towards the girl, who was leaning against a tree, panting.

"Oh, thank you!" she gasped. "It was terrible."

Major Wilbraham saw for the first time who it was he had rescued so opportunely. She was a girl of about twenty-one or two, fair-haired and blue-eyed, pretty in a rather colourless way.

"If you hadn't come!" she gasped.

"There, there," said Wilbraham soothingly. "It's all right now. I think, though, that we'd better get away from here. It's possible those fellows might come back."

A faint smile came to the girl's lips. "I don't think they will—not after the way you hit them. Oh, it was splendid of you!"

Major Wilbraham blushed under the warmth of her glance of admiration. "Nothin' at all," he said indistinctly. "All in day's work. Lady being annoyed. Look here, if you take my arm, can you walk? It's been a nasty shock, I know."

"I'm all right now," said the girl. However, she took the proffered arm. She was still rather shaky. She glanced behind her at the house as they emerged through the gate.

"I can't understand it," she murmured. "That's clearly an empty house."

"It's empty, right enough," agreed the major, looking up at the shuttered windows and general air of decay.

"And yet it *is* Whitefriars." She pointed to a half-obliterated name on the gate. "And Whitefriars was the place I was to go."

"Don't worry about anything now," said Wilbraham. "In a minute or two we'll be able to get a taxi. Then we'll drive somewhere and have a cup of coffee."

At the end of the lane they came out into a more frequented street, and by good fortune a taxi had just set down a fare at one of the houses. Wilbraham hailed it, gave an address to the driver and they got in.

"Don't try to talk," he admonished his companion. "Just lie back. You've had a nasty experience."

She smiled at him gratefully.

"By the way—er—my name is Wilbraham."

"Mine is Clegg—Freda Clegg."

Ten minutes later, Freda was sipping hot coffee and looking gratefully across a small table at her rescuer.

"It seems like a dream," she said. "A bad dream." She shuddered. "And only a short while ago I was wishing for something to happen—anything! Oh, I don't like adventures."

"Tell me how it happened."

"Well, to tell you properly I shall have to talk a lot about myself, I'm afraid."

"An excellent subject," said Wilbraham, with a bow.

"I am an orphan. My father—he was a sea captain—died when I was eight. My mother died three years ago. I work in the city. I am with the Vacuum Gas Company—a clerk. One evening last week I found a gentleman waiting to see me when I returned to my lodgings. He was a lawyer, a Mr. Reid from Melbourne.

"He was very polite and asked me several questions about my family. He explained that he had known my father many years ago. In fact, he had transacted some legal business for him. Then he told me the object of his visit. 'Miss Clegg,' he said, 'I have reason to suppose that you might benefit as the result of a financial transaction entered into by your father several years before he died.' I was very much surprised, of course.

"'It is unlikely that you would ever have heard anything of the matter,' he explained. 'John Clegg never took the affair seriously, I fancy. However, it has materialised unexpectedly, but I am afraid any claim you might put in would depend on your ownership of certain papers. These papers would be part of your father's estate, and of course it is possible that they have been destroyed as worthless. Have you kept any of your father's papers?'

"I explained that my mother had kept various things of my father's in an old sea chest. I had looked through it cursorily, but had discovered nothing of interest.

"'You would hardly be likely to recognise the importance of these documents, perhaps,' he said, smiling.

"Well, I went to the chest, took out the few papers it contained and brought them to him. He looked at them, but said it was impossible to say off-hand what might or might not be connected with the matter in question. He would take them away with him and would communicate with me if anything turned up.

"By the last post on Saturday I received a letter from him in which he suggested that I come to his house to discuss the matter. He gave me the address: Whitefriars, Friars Lane, Hampstead. I was to be there at a quarter to eleven this morning.

"I was a little late finding the place. I hurried through the gate and up towards the house, when suddenly those two dreadful men sprang at me from the bushes. I hadn't time to cry out. One man put his hand over my mouth. I wrenched my head free and screamed for help. Luckily you heard me. If it hadn't been for you——" She stopped. Her looks were more eloquent than further words.

"Very glad I happened to be on the spot. By Gad, I'd like to get hold of those two brutes. You'd never seen them before, I suppose?"

She shook her head. "What do you think it means?"

"Difficult to say. But one thing seems pretty sure. There's something someone wants among your father's papers. This man Reid told you a cock-and-bull story so as to get the opportunity of looking through them. Evidently what he wanted wasn't there."

"Oh!" said Freda. "I wonder. When I got home on Saturday I thought my things had been tampered with. To tell you the truth, I suspected my landlady of having pried about in my room out of curiosity. But now——"

"Depend upon it, that's it. Someone gained admission to your room and searched it, without finding what he was after. He suspected that you knew the value of this paper, whatever it was, and that you carried it about on your person. So he planned this ambush. If you had it with you, it would have been taken from you. If not, you would have been held prisoner while he tried to make you tell where it was hidden."

"But what can it possibly *be*?" cried Freda.

"I don't know. But it must be something pretty good for him to go to this length."

"It doesn't seem possible."

"Oh, I don't know. Your father was a sailor. He went to out-of-the-way places. He might have come across something the value of which he never knew."

"Do you really think so?" A pink flush of excitement showed in the girl's pale cheeks.

"I do indeed. The question is, what shall we do next? You don't want to go to the police, I suppose?"

"Oh, no, please."

"I'm glad you say that. I don't see what good the police could do, and it would only mean unpleasantness for you. Now I suggest that you allow me to give you lunch somewhere and that I then accompany you back to your lodgings, so as to be sure you reach them safely. And then, we might have a look for the paper. Because, you know, it must be somewhere."

"Father may have destroyed it himself."

"He may, of course, but the other side evidently doesn't think so, and that looks hopeful for us."

"What do you think it can be? Hidden treasure?"

"By jove, it might be!" exclaimed Major Wilbraham, all the boy in him rising joyfully to the suggestion. "But now, Miss Clegg, lunch!"

They had a pleasant meal together. Wilbraham told Freda all about his life in East Africa. He described elephant hunts, and the girl was thrilled. When they had finished, he insisted on taking her home in a taxi.

Her lodgings were near Notting Hill Gate. On arriving there, Freda had a brief conversation with her landlady. She returned to Wilbraham and took him up to the second floor, where she had a tiny bedroom and sitting-room.

"It's exactly as we thought," she said. "A man came on Saturday morning to see about laying a new electric cable; he told her there was a fault in the wiring in my room. He was there some time."

"Show me this chest of your father's," said Wilbraham.

Freda showed him a brass-bound box. "You see," she said, raising the lid, "it's empty."

The soldier nodded thoughtfully. "And there are no papers anywhere else?"

"I'm sure there aren't. Mother kept everything in here."

Wilbraham examined the inside of the chest. Suddenly he uttered an exclamation. "Here's a slit in the lining." Carefully he inserted his hand, feeling about. A slight crackle rewarded him. "Something's slipped down behind."

In another minute he had drawn out his find. A piece of dirty paper folded several times. He smoothed it out on the table; Freda was looking over his shoulder. She uttered an exclamation of disappointment.

"It's just a lot of queer marks."

"Why, the thing's in Swahili. *Swahili*, of all things!" cried Major Wilbraham. "East African native dialect, you know."

"How extraordinary!" said Freda. "Can you read it, then?"

"Rather. But what an amazing thing." He took the paper to the window.

"Is it anything?" asked Freda tremulously. Wilbraham read the thing through twice, and then came back to the girl. "Well," he said, with a chuckle, "here's your hidden treasure, all right."

"Hidden treasure? Not *really*? You mean Spanish gold—a sunken galleon—that sort of thing?"

"Not quite so romantic as that, perhaps. But it comes to the same thing. This paper gives the hiding-place of a cache of ivory."

"Ivory?" said the girl, astonished.

"Yes. Elephants, you know. There's a law about the number you're allowed to shoot. Some hunter got away with breaking that law on a grand scale. They were on his trail and he cached the stuff. There's a thundering lot of it—and this gives fairly clear directions how to find it. Look here, we'll have to go after this, you and I."

"You mean there's really a lot of money in it?"

"Quite a nice little fortune for you."

"But how did that paper come to be among my father's things?"

Wilbraham shrugged. "Maybe the Johnny was dying or something. He may have written the thing down in Swahili for protection and given it to your father, who possibly had befriended him in some way. Your father, not being able to read it, attached no importance to it. That's only a guess on my part, but I dare say it's not far wrong."

Freda gave a sigh. "How frightfully exciting!"

"The thing is—what to do with the precious document," said Wilbraham. "I don't like leaving it here. They might come and have another look. I suppose you wouldn't entrust it to me?"

"Of course I would. But—mightn't it be dangerous for you?" she faltered.

"I'm a tough nut," said Wilbraham grimly. "You needn't worry about me." He folded up the paper and put it in his pocket-book. "May I come to see you to-morrow evening?" he asked. "I'll have worked out a plan by then, and I'll look up the places on my map. What time do you get back from the city?"

"I get back about half-past six."

"Capital. We'll have a powwow and then perhaps you'll let me take you out to dinner. We ought to celebrate. So long, then. To-morrow at half-past six."

Major Wilbraham arrived punctually on the following day. He rang the bell and inquired for Miss Clegg. A maid-servant had answered the door.

"Miss Clegg? She's out."

"Oh!" Wilbraham did not like to suggest that he come in and wait. "I'll call back presently," he said.

He hung about in the street opposite, expecting every minute to see Freda tripping towards him. The minutes passed. Quarter to seven. Seven. Quarter-past seven. Still no Freda. A feeling of uneasiness swept over him. He went back to the house and rang the bell again.

"Look here," he said, "I had an appointment with Miss Clegg at half-past six. Are you sure she isn't in or hasn't—er—left any message?"

"Are you Major Wilbraham?" asked the servant.

"Yes."

"Then there's a note for you. It come by hand."

Wilbraham took it from her and tore it open. It ran as follows:

> Dear Major Wilbraham,—Something rather strange has happened. I won't write more now, but will you meet me at Whitefriars? Go there as soon as you get this.
>
> Yours sincerely,
>
> Freda Clegg

Wilbraham drew his brows together as he thought rapidly. His hand drew a letter absent-mindedly from his pocket. It was to his tailor. "I wonder," he said to the maid-servant, "if you could let me have a stamp."

"I expect Mrs. Parkins could oblige you."

She returned in a moment with the stamp. It was paid for with a shilling. In another minute Wilbraham was walking towards the tube station, dropping the envelope in a box as he passed.

Freda's letter had made him most uneasy. What could have taken the girl, alone, to the scene of yesterday's sinister encounter?

He shook his head. Of all the foolish things to do! Had Reid reappeared? Had he somehow or other prevailed upon the girl to trust him? What had taken her to Hampstead?

He looked at his watch. Nearly half-past seven. She would have counted on his starting at half-past six. An hour late. Too much. If only she had had the sense to give him some hint.

The letter puzzled him. Somehow its independent tone was not characteristic of Freda Clegg.

It was ten minutes to eight when he reached Friars Lane. It was getting dark. He looked sharply about him; there was no one in sight. Gently he pushed the rickety gate so that it swung noiselessly on its hinges. The drive was deserted. The house was dark. He went up the path cautiously, keeping a look out from side to side. He did not intend to be caught by surprise.

Suddenly he stopped. Just for a minute a chink of light had shone through one of the shutters. The house was not empty. There was someone inside.

Softly Wilbraham slipped into the bushes and worked his way round to the back of the house. At last he found what he was looking for. One of the windows on the ground floor was unfastened. It was the window of a kind of scullery. He raised the sash, flashed a torch (he had bought it at a shop on the way over) around the deserted interior and climbed in.

Carefully he opened the scullery door. There was no sound. He flashed the torch once more. A kitchen—empty. Outside the kitchen were half a dozen steps and a door evidently leading to the front part of the house.

He pushed open the door and listened. Nothing. He slipped through. He was now in the front hall. Still there was no sound. There was a door to the right and a door to the left. He chose the right-hand door, listened for a time, then turned the handle. It gave. Inch by inch he opened the door and stepped inside.

Again he flashed the torch. The room was unfurnished and bare.

Just at that moment he heard a sound behind him, whirled round—too late. Something came down on his head and he pitched forward into unconsciousness. . . .

How much time elapsed before he regained consciousness Wilbraham had no idea. He returned painfully to life, his head aching. He tried to move and found it impossible. He was bound with ropes.

His wits came back to him suddenly. He remembered now. He had been hit on the head.

A faint light from a gas jet high up on the wall showed him that he was in a small cellar. He looked around and his heart gave a leap. A few feet away lay Freda, bound like himself. Her eyes were closed, but even as he watched her anxiously, she sighed and they opened. Her bewildered gaze fell on him and joyous recognition leaped into them.

"You, too!" she said. "What has happened?"

"I've let you down badly," said Wilbraham. "Tumbled headlong into the trap. Tell me, did you send me a note asking me to meet you here?"

The girl's eyes opened in astonishment. "*I?* But you sent *me* one."

"Oh, I sent you one, did I?"

"Yes. I got it at the office. It asked me to meet you here instead of at home."

"Same method for both of us," he groaned, and he explained the situation.

"I see," said Freda. "Then the idea was——?"

"To get the paper. We must have been followed yesterday. That's how they got on to me."

"And—have they got it?" asked Freda.

"Unfortunately, I can't feel and see," said the soldier, regarding his bound hands ruefully.

And then they both started. For a voice spoke, a voice that seemed to come from the empty air.

"Yes, thank you," it said. "I've got it, all right. No mistake about that."

The unseen voice made them both shiver.

"Mr. Reid," murmured Freda.

"Mr. Reid is one of my names, my dear young lady," said the voice. "But only one of them. I have a great many. Now, I am sorry to say that you two have interfered with my plans—a thing I never allow. Your discovery of this house is a serious matter. You have not told the police about it yet, but you might do so in the future.

"I very much fear that I cannot trust you in the matter. You might promise—but promises are seldom kept. And, you see, this house is very useful to me. It is, you might say, my clearing house. The house from which there is no return. From here you pass on—elsewhere. You, I am sorry to say, are so passing on. Regrettable—but necessary."

The voice paused for a brief second, then resumed: "No bloodshed. I abhor bloodshed. My method is much simpler. And really not too painful, so I understand. Well, I must be getting along. Good-evening to you both."

"Look here!" It was Wilbraham who spoke. "Do what you like to me, but this young lady has done nothing—nothing. It can't hurt you to let her go."

But there was no answer.

At that moment there came a cry from Freda. "The water—the water!"

Wilbraham twisted himself painfully and followed the direction of her eyes. From a hole up near the ceiling a steady trickle of water was pouring in.

Freda gave a hysterical cry. "They're going to drown us!"

The perspiration broke out on Wilbraham's brow. "We're not done yet," he said. "We'll shout for help. Surely somebody will hear. Now, both together."

They yelled and shouted at the top of their voices. Not till they were hoarse did they stop.

"No use, I'm afraid," said Wilbraham sadly. "We're too far underground and I expect the doors are muffled. After all, if we could be heard, I've no doubt that brute would have gagged us."

"Oh!" cried Freda. "And it's all my fault. I got you into this."

"Don't worry about that, little girl. It's you I'm thinking about. I've been in tight corners before now and got out of them. Don't you lose heart. I'll get you out of this. We've plenty of time. At the rate that water's flowing in, it will be hours before the worst happens."

"How wonderful you are!" said Freda. "I've never met anybody like you—except in books."

"Nonsense—just common sense. Now, I've got to loosen these infernal ropes."

At the end of a quarter of an hour, by dint of straining and twisting, Wilbraham had the satisfaction of feeling that his bonds were appreciably loosened. He managed to bend his head down and his wrists up till he was able to attack the knots with his teeth.

Once his hands were free, the rest was only a matter of time. Cramped, stiff, but free, he bent over the girl. A minute later she also was free.

So far the water was only up to their ankles.

"And now," said the soldier, "to get out of here."

The door of the cellar was up a few stairs. Major Wilbraham examined it.

"No difficulty here," he said. "Flimsy stuff. It will soon give at the hinges." He set his shoulders to it and heaved.

There was the cracking of wood—a crash, and the door burst from its hinges.

Outside was a flight of stairs. At the top was another door—a very different affair—of solid wood, barred with iron.

"A bit more difficult, this," said Wilbraham. "Hallo, here's a piece of luck. It's unlocked."

He pushed it open, peered round it, then beckoned the girl to come on. They emerged into a passage behind the kitchen. In another moment they were standing under the stars in Friars Lane.

"Oh!" Freda gave a little sob. "Oh, how dreadful it's been!"

"My poor darling." He caught her in his arms. "You've been so wonderfully brave. Freda—darling angel—could you ever—I mean, would you—I love you, Freda. Will you marry me?"

After a suitable interval, highly satisfactory to both parties, Major Wilbraham said, with a chuckle:

"And what's more, we've still got the secret of the ivory cache."

"But they took it from you!"

The major chuckled again. "That's just what they didn't do! You see, I wrote out a spoof copy, and before joining you here to-night, I put the real thing in a letter I was sending to my tailor and posted it. They've got the spoof copy—and I wish them joy of it! Do you know what we'll do, sweetheart! We'll go to East Africa for our honeymoon and hunt out the cache."

Mr. Parker Pyne left his office and climbed two flights of stairs. Here in a room at the top of the house sat Mrs. Oliver, the sensational novelist, now a member of Mr. Pyne's staff.

Mr. Parker Pyne tapped at the door and entered. Mrs. Oliver sat at a table on which were a typewriter, several notebooks, a general confusion of loose manuscripts and a large bag of apples.

"A very good story, Mrs. Oliver," said Mr. Parker Pyne genially.

"It went off well?" said Mrs. Oliver. "I'm glad."

"That water-in-the-cellar business," said Mr. Parker Pyne. "You don't think, on a future occasion, that something more original—perhaps?" He made the suggestion with proper diffidence.

Mrs. Oliver shook her head and took an apple from the bag. "I think not, Mr. Pyne. You see, people are used to reading about such things. Water rising in a cellar, poison gas, et cetera. Knowing about it beforehand gives it an extra thrill when it happens to oneself. The public is conservative, Mr. Pyne; it likes the old well-worn gadgets."

"Well, you should know," admitted Mr. Parker Pyne, mindful of the authoress's forty-six successful works of fiction, all best sellers in England and America, and freely translated into French, German, Italian, Hungarian, Finnish, Japanese, and Abyssinian. "How about expenses?"

Mrs. Oliver drew a paper towards her. "Very moderate, on the whole. The two darkies, Percy and Jerry, wanted very little. Young Lorrimer, the actor, was willing to enact the part of Mr. Reid for five guineas. The cellar speech was a phonograph record, of course."

"Whitefriars has been extremely useful to me," said Mr. Pyne. "I bought it for a song and it has already been the scene of eleven exciting dramas."

"Oh, I forgot," said Mrs. Oliver. "Johnny's wages. Five shillings."

"Johnny?"

"Yes. The boy who poured the water from the watering cans through the hole in the wall."

"Ah, yes. By the way, Mrs. Oliver, how did you happen to know Swahili?"

"I didn't."

"I see. The British Museum, perhaps?"

"No. Delfridge's Information Bureau."

"How marvellous are the resources of modern commerce!" he murmured.

"The only thing that worries me," said Mrs. Oliver, "is

that those two young people won't find any cache when they get there."

"One cannot have everything in this world," said Mr. Parker Pyne. "They will have had a honeymoon."

Mrs. Wilbraham was sitting in a deck-chair. Her husband was writing a letter. "What's the date, Freda?"

"The sixteenth."

"The sixteenth. By jove!"

"What is it, dear?"

"Nothing. I just remembered a chap named Jones."

However happily married, there are some things one never tells.

"Dash it all," thought Major Wilbraham, "I ought to have called at that place and got my money back." And then, being a fair-minded man, he looked at the other side of the question. "After all, it was I who broke the bargain. I suppose if I'd gone to see Jones something would have happened. And, anyway, as it turns out, if I hadn't been going to see Jones, I should never have heard Freda cry for help, and we might never have met. So, indirectly, perhaps they have a right to that fifty pounds!"

Mrs. Wilbraham was also following out a train of thought. "What a silly little fool I was to believe in that advertisement and pay those people three guineas. Of course, they never did anything for it and nothing ever happened. If I'd only known what was coming—first Mr. Reid, and then the queer, romantic way that Charlie came into my life. And to think that *but for pure chance* I might never have met him!"

She turned and smiled adoringly at her husband.

THE CASE OF THE DISTRESSED LADY

The buzzer on Mr. Parker Pyne's desk purred discreetly. "Yes?" said the great man.

"A young lady wishes to see you," announced his secretary. "She has no appointment."

"You may send her in, Miss Lemon." A moment later he was shaking hands with his visitor. "Good-morning," he said. "Do sit down."

The girl sat down and looked at Mr. Parker Pyne. She was a pretty girl and quite young. Her hair was dark and wavy with a row of curls at the nape of the neck. She was beautifully turned out from the white knitted cap on her head to the cobweb stockings and dainty shoes. Clearly she was nervous.

"You are Mr. Parker Pyne?" she asked.

"I am."

"The one who—who—advertises?"

"The one who advertises."

"You say that if people aren't—aren't happy—to—to come to you."

"Yes."

She took the plunge. "Well, I'm frightfully unhappy. So I thought I'd come along and just—and just see."

Mr. Parker Pyne waited. He felt there was more to come.

"I—I'm in frightful trouble." She clenched her hands nervously.

"So I see," said Mr. Parker Pyne. "Do you think you could tell me about it?"

That, it seemed, was what the girl was by no means sure of. She stared at Mr. Parker Pyne with a desperate intentness. Suddenly she spoke with a rush.

"Yes, I will tell you. I've made up my mind now. I've been nearly crazy with worry. I didn't know what to do or whom to go to. And then I saw your advertisement. I thought it was probably just a ramp, but it stayed in my mind. It sounded so comforting, somehow. And then I thought—well, it would do no harm to come and *see*. I could always make an excuse and get away again if I didn't—well, it didn't——"

"Quite so; quite so," said Mr. Pyne.

"You see," said the girl, "it means—well, *trusting* somebody."

"And you feel you can trust me?" he said, smiling.

"It's odd," said the girl with unconscious rudeness, "but I do. Without knowing anything about you! I'm *sure* I can trust you."

"I can assure you," said Mr. Pyne, "that your trust will not be misplaced."

"Then," said the girl, "I'll tell you about it. My name is Daphne St. John."

"Yes, Miss St. John."

"Mrs. I'm—I'm married."

"Pshaw!" muttered Mr. Pyne, annoyed with himself as he noted the platinum circlet on the third finger of her left hand. "Stupid of me."

"If I weren't married," said the girl, "I shouldn't mind so much. I mean, it wouldn't matter so much. It's the thought of Gerald—— Well, here—here's what all the trouble's about!"

She dived in her bag, took something out and flung it down on the desk where, gleaming and flashing, it rolled over to Mr. Parker Pyne.

It was a platinum ring with a large solitaire diamond.

Mr. Pyne picked it up, took it to the window, tested it on the pane, applied a jeweller's lens to his eye and examined it closely.

"An exceedingly fine diamond," he remarked, coming back to the table; "worth, I should say, about two thousand pounds at least."

"Yes. And it's stolen! I stole it! And I don't know what to do."

"Dear me!" said Mr. Parker Pyne. "This is very interesting."

His client broke down and sobbed into an inadequate handkerchief.

"Now, now," said Mr. Pyne. "Everything's going to be all right."

The girl dried her eyes and sniffed. "Is it?" she said. "Oh, *is* it?"

"Of course it is. Now, just tell me the whole story."

"Well, it began by my being hard up. You see, I'm frightfully extravagant. And Gerald gets so annoyed about it. Gerald's my husband. He's a lot older than I am, and he's got very—well, very austere ideas. He thinks running into debt is dreadful. So I didn't tell him. And I went over to Le Touquet with some friends and I thought perhaps I might be lucky at chemmy and get straight again. I did win at first. And then I lost, and then I thought I must go on. And I went on. And—and——"

"Yes, yes," said Mr. Parker Pyne. "You need not go into details. You were in a worse plight than ever. That is right, is it not?"

Daphne St. John nodded. "And by then, you see, I simply couldn't tell Gerald. Because he hates gambling. Oh, I was in an awful mess. Well, we went down to stay with the Dortheimers near Cobham. He's frightfully rich, of course. His wife, Naomi, was at school with me. She's pretty and a dear. While we were there, the setting of this ring got loose. On the morning we were leaving, she asked me to take it up to town and drop it at her jeweller's in Bond Street." She paused.

"And now we come to the difficult part," said Mr. Pyne helpfully. "Go on, Mrs. St. John."

"You won't ever tell, will you?" demanded the girl pleadingly.

"My clients' confidences are sacred. And anyway, Mrs. St. John, you have told me so much already that I could probably finish the story for myself."

"That's true. All right. But I hate saying it—it sounds so awful. I went to Bond Street. There's another shop there —Viro's. They—copy jewellery. Suddenly I lost my head. I took the ring in and said I wanted an exact copy; I said I was going abroad and didn't want to take real jewellery with me. They seemed to think it quite natural.

"Well, I got the paste replica—it was so good you couldn't have told it from the original—and I sent it off by registered post to Lady Dortheimer. I had a box with the jeweller's name on it, so that was all right, and I made a professional-looking parcel. And then I—I—pawned the real one." She hid her face in her hands. "How could I? How *could* I? I was just a low, mean, common thief."

Mr. Parker Pyne coughed. "I do not think you have quite finished," he said.

"No, I haven't. This, you understand, was about six weeks ago. I paid off all my debts and got square again, but, of course, I was miserable all the time. And then an old cousin of mine died and I came into some money. The first thing I did was to redeem the wretched ring. Well, that's all right; here it is. But something terribly difficult has happened."

"Yes?"

"We've had a quarrel with the Dortheimers. It's over some shares that Sir Reuben persuaded Gerald to buy. He was terribly let in over them and he told Sir Reuben what he thought of him—and oh, it's all dreadful! And now, you see, I can't get the ring back."

"Couldn't you send it to Lady Dortheimer anonymously?"

"That gives the whole thing away. She'll examine her own ring, find it's a fake and guess at once what I've done."

"You say she is a friend of yours. What about telling her the whole truth—throwing yourself on her mercy?"

Mrs. St. John shook her head. "We're not such friends as that. Where money or jewellery is concerned, Naomi's as hard as nails. Perhaps she couldn't prosecute me if I gave the ring back, but she could tell everyone what I've done and I'd be ruined. Gerald would know and he would never forgive me. Oh, how awful everything is!" She began to cry again. "I've thought and I've thought, and I can't see *what* to do! Oh, Mr. Pyne, can't you do anything?"

"Several things," said Mr. Parker Pyne.

"You can? Really?"

"Certainly. I suggested the simplest way because in my long experience I have always found it the best. It avoids unlooked-for complications. Still, I see the force of your objections. At present no one knows of this unfortunate occurrence but yourself?"

"And you," said Mrs. St. John.

"Oh, I do not count. Well, then, your secret is safe at present. All that is needed is to exchange the rings in some unsuspicious manner."

"That's it," the girl said eagerly.

"That should not be difficult. We must take a little time to consider the best method——"

She interrupted him. "But there is no time! That's what's driving me nearly crazy. She's going to have the ring reset."

"How do you know?"

"Just by chance. I was lunching with a woman the other

day and I admired a ring she had on—a big emerald. She said it was the newest thing—and that Naomi Dortheimer was going to have her diamond reset that way."

"Which means that we shall have to act quickly," said Mr. Pyne thoughtfully.

"Yes, yes."

"It means gaining admission to the house—and if possible not in a menial capacity. Servants have little chance of handling valuable rings. Have you any ideas yourself, Mrs. St. John?"

"Well, Naomi is giving a big party on Wednesday. And this friend of mine mentioned that she had been looking for some exhibition dancers. I don't know if anything has been settled——"

"I think that can be managed," said Mr. Parker Pyne. "If the matter is already settled it will be more expensive, that is all. One thing more, do you happen to know where the main light switch is situated?"

"As it happens I *do* know that, because a fuse blew out late one night when the servants had all gone to bed. It's a box at the back of the hall—inside a little cupboard."

At Mr. Parker Pyne's request she drew him a sketch.

"And now," said Mr. Parker Pyne, "everything is going to be all right, so don't worry, Mrs. St. John. What about the ring? Shall I take it now, or would you rather keep it till Wednesday?"

"Well, perhaps I'd better keep it."

"Now, no more worry, mind you," Mr. Parker Pyne admonished her.

"And your—fee?" she asked timidly.

"That can stand over for the moment. I will let you know on Wednesday what expenses have been necessary. The fee will be nominal, I assure you."

He conducted her to the door, then rang the buzzer on his desk.

"Send Claude and Madeleine here."

Claude Luttrell was one of the handsomest specimens of lounge-lizard to be found in England. Madeleine de Sara was the most seductive of vamps.

Mr. Parker Pyne surveyed them with approval. "My children," he said, "I have a job for you. You are going to be internationally famous exhibition dancers. Now, attend to this carefully, Claude, and mind you get it right . . ."

Lady Dortheimer was fully satisfied with the arrangements for her ball. She surveyed the floral decorations and approved, gave a few last orders to the butler, and remarked to her husband that so far nothing had gone wrong!

It was a slight disappointment that Michael and Juanita, the dancers from the Red Admiral, had been unable to fulfill their contract at the last moment, owing to Juanita's spraining her ankle, but instead, two new dancers were being sent (so ran the story over the telephone) who had created a furore in Paris.

The dancers duly arrived and Lady Dortheimer approved. The evening went splendidly. Jules and Sanchia did their turn, and most sensational it was. A wild Spanish Revolution dance. Then a dance called the Degenerate's Dream. Then an exquisite exhibition of modern dancing.

The "cabaret" over, normal dancing was resumed. The handsome Jules requested a dance with Lady Dortheimer. They floated away. Never had Lady Dortheimer had such a perfect partner.

Sir Reuben was searching for the seductive Sanchia—in vain. She was not in the ballroom.

She was, as a matter of fact, out in the deserted hall near a small box, with her eyes fixed on the jewelled watch which she wore round her wrist.

"You are not English—you cannot be English—to dance as you do," murmured Jules into Lady Dortheimer's ear. "You are the sprite, the spirit of the wind. *Droushcka petrovka navarouchi.*"

"What is that language?"

"Russian," said Jules mendaciously. "I say something to you in Russian that I dare not say in English."

Lady Dortheimer closed her eyes. Jules pressed her closer to him.

Suddenly the lights went out. In the darkness Jules bent and kissed the hand that lay on his shoulder. As she made to draw it away, he caught it, raised it to his lips again. Somehow a ring slipped from her finger into his hand.

To Lady Dortheimer it seemed only a second before the lights went on again. Jules was smiling at her.

"Your ring," he said. "It slipped off. You permit?" He replaced it on her finger. His eyes said a number of things while he was doing it.

Sir Reuben was talking about the main switch. "Some idiot. Practical joke, I suppose."

Lady Dortheimer was not interested. Those few minutes of darkness had been very pleasant.

Mr. Parker Pyne arrived at his office on Thursday morning to find Mrs. St. John already awaiting him.

"Show her in," said Mr. Pyne.

"Well?" She was all eagerness.

"You look pale," he said accusingly.

She shook her head. "I couldn't sleep last night. I was wondering——"

"Now, here is the little bill for expenses. Train fares, costumes, and fifty pounds to Michael and Juanita. Sixty-five pounds, seventeen shillings."

"Yes, yes! But about last night—was it all right? Did it happen?"

Mr. Parker Pyne looked at her in surprise. "My dear young lady, naturally it is all right. I took it for granted that you understood that."

"What a relief! I was afraid——"

Mr. Parker Pyne shook his head reproachfully. "Failure is a word not tolerated in this establishment. If I do not think I can succeed I refuse to undertake a case. If I do take a case, its success is practically a foregone conclusion."

"She's really got her ring back and suspects nothing?"

"Nothing whatever. The operation was most delicately conducted."

Daphne St. John sighed. "You don't know the load off my mind. What were you saying about expenses?"

"Sixty-five pounds, seventeen shillings."

Mrs. St. John opened her bag and counted out the money. Mr. Parker Pyne thanked her and wrote out a receipt.

"But your fee?" murmured Daphne. "This is only for expenses."

"In this case there is no fee."

"Oh, Mr. Pyne! I couldn't, *really*!"

"My dear young lady, I insist. I will not touch a penny. It would be against my principles. Here is your receipt. And now——"

With the smile of a happy conjurer bringing off a successful trick, he drew a small box from his pocket and pushed it across the table. Daphne opened it. Inside, to all appearances, lay the identical diamond ring.

"Brute!" said Mrs. St. John, making a face at it. "How I hate you! I've a good mind to throw you out of the window."

"I shouldn't do that," said Mr. Pyne. "It might surprise people."

"You're quite sure it isn't the real one?" said Daphne.

"No, no! The one you showed me the other day is safely on Lady Dortheimer's finger."

"Then that's all right." Daphne rose with a happy laugh.

"Curious your asking me that," said Mr. Parker Pyne. "Of course Claude, poor fellow, hasn't many brains. He might easily have got muddled. So, to make sure, I had an expert look at this thing this morning."

Mrs. St. John sat down again rather suddenly. "Oh! And he said?"

"That it was an extraordinary good imitation," said Mr. Parker Pyne, beaming. "First-class work. So that sets your mind at rest, doesn't it?"

Mrs. St. John started to say something, then stopped. She was staring at Mr. Parker Pyne.

The latter resumed his seat behind the desk and looked at her benevolently. "The cat who pulled the chestnuts out of the fire," he said dreamily. "Not a pleasant rôle. Not a rôle I should care to have any of my staff undertake. Excuse me. Did you say anything?"

"I—no, nothing."

"Good. I want to tell you a little story, Mrs. St. John. It concerns a young lady. A fair-haired young lady, I think. She is not married. Her name is not St. John. Her Christian name is not Daphne. On the contrary, her name is Ernestine Richards, and until recently she was secretary to Lady Dortheimer.

"Well, one day the setting of Lady Dortheimer's diamond

ring became loose and Miss Richards brought it up to town to have it fixed. Quite like your story here, is it not? The same idea occurred to Miss Richards that occurred to you. She had the ring copied. But she was a far-sighted young lady. She saw a day coming when Lady Dortheimer would discover the substitution. When that happened, she would remember who had taken the ring to town and Miss Richards would be instantly suspected.

"So what happened? First, I fancy, Miss Richards invested in a La Merveilleuse transformation—Number Seven side parting, I think"—his eyes rested innocently on his client's wavy locks—"shade dark brown. Then she called on me. She showed me the ring, allowed me to satisfy myself that it was genuine, thereby disarming suspicion on my part. That done, and a plan of substitution arranged, the young lady took the ring to the jeweller, who, in due course, returned it to Lady Dortheimer.

"Yesterday evening the other ring, the false ring, was hurriedly handed over at the last minute at Waterloo Station. Quite rightly, Miss Richards did not consider that Mr. Luttrell was likely to be an authority on diamonds. But just to satisfy myself that everything was above board I arranged for a friend of mine, a diamond merchant, to be on the train. He looked at the ring and pronounced at once, 'This is not a real diamond; it is an excellent paste replica.'

"You see the point, of course, Mrs. St. John? When Lady Dortheimer discovered her loss, what would she remember? The charming young dancer who slipped the ring off her finger when the lights went out! She would make inquiries and find that the dancers originally engaged were bribed not to come. If matters were traced back to my office, my story of a Mrs. St. John would seem feeble in the extreme. Lady Dortheimer never knew a Mrs. St. John. The story would sound a flimsy fabrication.

"Now you see, don't you, that I could not allow that? And so my friend Claude replaced on Lady Dortheimer's finger *the same ring that he took off.*" Mr. Parker Pyne's smile was less benevolent now.

"You see why I could not take a fee? I guarantee to give happiness. Clearly I have not made *you* happy. I will say just one thing more. You are young; possibly this is your first attempt at anything of the kind. Now I, on the contrary, am comparatively advanced in years, and I have had a long experience in the compilation of statistics. From that experience I can assure you that in eighty-seven per cent. of cases dishonesty does not pay. Eighty-seven per cent. Think of it!"

With a brusque movement the pseudo Mrs. St. John rose. "You oily old brute!" she said. "Leading me on! Making me pay expenses! And all the time——" She choked, and rushed toward the door.

"Your ring," said Mr. Parker Pyne, holding it out to her.

She snatched it from him, looked at it and flung it out of the open window.

A door banged and she was gone.

Mr. Parker Pyne was looking out of the window with some interest. "As I thought," he said. "Considerable surprise has been created. The gentleman selling Dismal Desmonds does not know what to make of it."

THE CASE OF THE DISCONTENTED HUSBAND

Undoubtedly one of Mr. Parker Pyne's greatest assets was his sympathetic manner. It was a manner that invited confidence. He was well acquainted with the kind of paralysis that descended on clients as soon as they got inside his office. It was Mr. Pyne's task to pave the way for the necessary disclosures.

On this particular morning he sat facing a new client, a Mr. Reginald Wade. Mr. Wade, he deduced at once, was the inarticulate type. The type that finds it hard to put into words anything connected with the emotions.

He was a tall, broadly-built man with mild, pleasant blue eyes and a well-tanned complexion. He sat pulling absent-mindedly at a little moustache while he looked at Mr. Parker Pyne with all the pathos of a dumb animal.

"Saw your advertisement, you know," he jerked. "Thought I might as well come along. Rum sort of show, but you never know, what?"

Mr. Parker Pyne interpreted these cryptic remarks correctly. "When things go badly, one is willing to take a chance," he suggested.

"That's it. That's it, exactly. I'm willing to take a chance—any chance. Things are in a bad way with me, Mr. Pyne. I don't know what to do about it. Difficult, you know; damned difficult."

"That," said Mr. Pyne, "is where I come in. I *do* know what to do! I am a specialist in every kind of human trouble."

"Oh, I say—bit of a tall order, that!"

"Not really. Human troubles are easily classified into a few main heads. There is ill health. There is boredom. There are wives who are in trouble over their husbands. There are husbands"—he paused—"who are in trouble over their wives."

"Matter of fact, you've hit it. You've hit it absolutely."

"Tell me about it," said Mr. Pyne.

"There's nothing much to tell. My wife wants me to give her a divorce so that she can marry another chap."

"Very common indeed in these days. Now you, I gather, don't see eye to eye with her in this business?"

"I'm fond of her," said Mr. Wade simply. "You see—well, I'm fond of her."

A simple and somewhat tame statement, but if Mr. Wade had said, "I adore her. I worship the ground she walks on. I would cut myself into little pieces for her," he could not have been more explicit to Mr. Parker Pyne.

"All the same, you know," went on Mr. Wade, "what can I do? I mean, a fellow's so helpless. If she prefers this other fellow—well, one's got to play the game; stand aside and all that."

"The proposal is that she should divorce you?"

"Of course. I couldn't let her be dragged through the divorce court."

Mr. Pyne looked at him thoughtfully. "But you come to me? Why?"

The other laughed in a shamefaced manner. "I don't know. You see, I'm not a clever chap. I can't think of things. I thought you might—well, suggest something. I've got six months, you see. She agreed to that. If at the end of six months she is still of the same mind—well, then, I get out. I thought you might give me a hint or two. At present everything I do annoys her.

"You see, Mr. Pyne, what it comes to is this: I'm not a clever chap! I like knocking balls about. I like a round of golf and a good set of tennis. I'm no good at music and art and such things. My wife's clever. She likes pictures and the opera and concerts, and naturally she gets bored with me. This other fellow—nasty long-haired chap—he knows all about these things. He can talk about them. I can't. In a way, I can understand a clever, beautiful woman getting fed up with an ass like me."

Mr. Parker Pyne groaned. "You have been married—how long? . . . Nine years? And I suppose you have adopted that attitude from the start. Wrong, my dear sir; disastrously wrong! Never adopt an apologetic attitude with a woman. She will take you at your own valuation—and you deserve it. You should have gloried in your athletic prowess. You should have spoken of art and music as 'all that nonsense my wife likes.' You should have condoled with her on not being able to play games better. The humble spirit, my dear sir, is a wash-out in matrimony! No woman can be expected to stand up against it. No wonder your wife has been unable to last the course."

Mr. Wade was looking at him in bewilderment. "Well," he said, "what do you think I ought to do?"

"That certainly is the question. Whatever you should have done nine years ago, it is too late now. New tactics must be adopted. Have you ever had any affairs with other women?"

"Certainly not."

"I should have said, perhaps, any light flirtations?"

"I never bothered about women much."

"A mistake. You must start now."

Mr. Wade looked alarmed. "Oh, look here, I couldn't really. I mean——"

"You will be put to no trouble in the matter. One of my staff will be supplied for the purpose. She will tell you what is required of you, and any attentions you pay her she will, of course, understand to be merely a matter of business."

Mr. Wade looked relieved. "That's better. But do you really think—I mean, it seems to me that Iris will be keener to get rid of me than ever."

"You do not understand human nature, Mr. Wade. Still less do you understand feminine human nature. At the present moment you are, from the feminine point of view, merely a waste product. Nobody wants you. What use has a woman for something that no one wants? None whatever. But take another angle. Suppose your wife discovers that you are looking forward to regaining your freedom as much as she is?"

"Then she ought to be pleased."

"She ought to be, perhaps, but she will not be! Moreover, she will see that you have attracted a fascinating young woman—a young woman who could pick and choose. Immediately your stock goes up. Your wife knows that all her friends will say it was you who tired of her and wished to marry a more attractive woman. That will annoy her."

"You think so?"

"I am sure of it. You will no longer be 'poor dear old Reggie.' You will be 'that sly dog Reggie.' All the difference in the world! Without relinquishing the other man, she will doubtless try to win you back. You will not be won. You will be sensible and repeat to her all her arguments. 'Much better to part.' 'Temperamentally unsuited.' You realise that while what she said was true—that you had never understood her—it is also true that *she* had never understood *you*. But we need not go into this now; you will be given full instructions when the time comes."

Mr. Wade seemed doubtful still. "You really think that this plan of yours will do the trick?" he asked dubiously.

"I will not say I am absolutely sure of it," said Mr. Parker Pyne cautiously. "There is a bare possibility that your wife may be so overwhelmingly in love with this other man that nothing you could say or do will affect her, but I consider that unlikely. She has probably been driven into this affair through boredom—boredom with the atmosphere of uncritical devotion and absolute fidelity with which you have most unwisely surrounded her. If you follow my instructions, the chances are, I should say, ninety-seven per cent. in your favour."

"Good enough," said Mr. Wade. "I'll do it. By the way—er—how much?"

"My fee is two hundred guineas, payable in advance."

Mr. Wade drew out a cheque book.

The grounds of Lorrimer Court were lovely in the afternoon sunshine. Iris Wade, lying on a long chair, made a delicious spot of colour. She was dressed in delicate shades of mauve and by skilful make-up managed to look much younger than her thirty-five years.

She was talking to her friend Mrs. Massington, whom she always found sympathetic. Both ladies were afflicted with athletic husbands who talked stocks and shares and golf alternately.

". . . And so one learns to live and let live," finished Iris.

"You're wonderful, darling," said Mrs. Massington, and added too quickly: "Tell me, who *is* this girl?"

Iris raised a weary shoulder. "Don't ask me! Reggie found her. She's Reggie's little friend! So amusing. You know he never looks at girls as a rule. He came to me and hemmed and hawed, and finally said he wanted to ask this Miss de Sara down for the week-end. Of course I laughed—I couldn't help it. *Reggie*, you know! Well, here she is."

"Where did he meet her?"

"I don't know. He was very vague about it all."

"Perhaps he's known her some time."

"Oh, I don't think so," said Mrs. Wade. "Of course," she went on, "I'm delighted—simply delighted. I mean, it makes it so much easier for me, as things are. Because I *have* been unhappy about Reggie; he's such a dear old thing. That's what I kept saying to Sinclair—that it would hurt Reggie so. But he insisted that Reggie would soon get over it; it looks as if he were right. Two days ago Reggie seemed heart-broken—and now he wants this girl down! As I say, I'm *amused*. I like to see Reggie enjoying himself. I fancy the poor fellow actually thought I might be jealous. Such an absurd idea! 'Of course,' I said, 'have your friend down.' Poor Reggie—as though a girl like that could ever care about him. She's just amusing herself."

"She's extremely attractive," said Mrs. Massington. "Almost dangerously so, if you know what I mean. The sort of girl who cares only for men. I don't feel, somehow, she can be a really nice girl."

"Probably not," said Mrs. Wade.

"She has marvellous clothes," said Mrs. Massington.

"Almost too exotic, don't you think?"

"But very expensive."

"Opulent. She's too opulent looking."

"Here they come," said Mrs. Massington.

Madeleine de Sara and Reggie Wade were walking across the lawn. They were laughing and talking together and seemed very happy. Madeleine flung herself into a chair, tore off the beret she was wearing and ran her hands through her exquisitely dark curls.

She was undeniably beautiful.

"We've had such a marvellous afternoon!" she cried. "I'm terribly hot. I must be looking too dreadful."

Reggie Wade started nervously at the sound of his cue. "You look—you look——" He gave a little laugh. "I won't say it," he finished.

Madeleine's eyes met his. It was a glance of complete understanding on her part. Mrs. Massington noted it alertly.

"You should play golf," said Madeleine to her hostess. "You miss such a lot. Why don't you take it up? I have a friend who did and became quite good, and she was a lot older than you."

"I don't care for that sort of thing," said Iris coldly.

"Are you bad at games? How rotten for you! It makes one feel so out of things. But really, Mrs. Wade, coaching nowadays is so good that almost anyone can play fairly well. I improved my tennis no end last summer. Of course I'm hopeless at golf."

"Nonsense!" said Reggie. "You only need coaching. Look how you were getting those brassie shots this afternoon."

"Because you showed me how. You're a wonderful teacher. Lots of people simply can't teach. But you've got the gift. It must be wonderful to be you—you can do everything."

"Nonsense. I'm no good—no use whatever." Reggie was confused.

"You must be very proud of him," said Madeleine, turning to Mrs. Wade. "How have you managed to keep him all these years? You must have been very clever. Or have you hidden him away?"

Her hostess made no reply. She picked up her book with a hand that trembled.

Reggie murmured something about changing, and went off.

"I do think it's so sweet of you to have me here," said Madeleine to her hostess. "Some women are so suspicious of their husbands' friends. I do think jealousy is absurd, don't you?"

"I do indeed. I should never dream of being jealous of Reggie."

"That's wonderful of you! Because anyone can see that he's a man who's frightfully attractive to women. It was a shock to me when I heard he was married. Why do all the attractive men get snapped up young?"

"I'm glad you find Reggie so attractive," said Mrs. Wade.

"Well, he is, isn't he? So good-looking, and so frightfully good at games. And that pretended indifference of his to women. That spurs us on, of course."

"I suppose you have a lot of men friends," said Mrs. Wade.

"Oh, yes. I like men better than women. Women are never really nice to me. I can't think why."

"Perhaps you are too nice to their husbands," said Mrs. Massington with a tinkly laugh.

"Well, one's sorry for people sometimes. So many nice men are tied to such dull wives. You know, 'arty' women and highbrow women. Naturally, the men want someone young and bright to talk to. I think the modern ideas of marriage and divorce are so sensible. Start again while one is still young with someone who shares one's tastes and ideas. It's better for everybody in the end. I mean, the highbrow wives probably pick up some long-haired creature of their own type who satisfies them. I think cutting your losses and starting again is a wise plan, don't you, Mrs. Wade?"

"Certainly."

A certain frostiness in the atmosphere seemed to penetrate Madeleine's consciousness. She murmured something about changing for tea and left them.

"Detestable creatures these modern girls are," said Mrs. Wade. "Not an idea in their heads."

"She's got one idea in hers, Iris," said Mrs. Massington. "That girl's in love with Reggie."

"Nonsense!"

"She is. I saw the way she looked at him just now. She doesn't care a pin whether he's married or not. She means to have him. Disgusting, I call it."

Mrs. Wade was silent a moment, then she laughed uncertainly. "After all," she said, "what does it matter?"

Presently Mrs. Wade, too, went upstairs. Her husband was in his dressing-room changing. He was singing.

"Enjoyed yourself, dear?" said Mrs. Wade.

"Oh, er—rather, yes."

"I'm glad. I want you to be happy."

"Yes, rather."

Acting a part was not Reggie Wade's strong point, but as it happened, the acute embarrassment occasioned by his fancying he was doing so did just as well. He avoided his wife's eye and jumped when she spoke to him. He felt ashamed; hated the farce of it all. Nothing could have produced a better effect. He was the picture of conscious guilt.

"How long have you known her?" asked Mrs. Wade suddenly.

"Er—who?"

"Miss de Sara, of course."

"Well, I don't quite know. I mean—oh, some time."

"Really? You never mentioned her."

"Didn't I? I suppose I forgot."

"Forgot indeed!" said Mrs. Wade. She departed with a whisk of mauve draperies.

After tea Mr. Wade showed Miss de Sara the rose garden. They walked across the lawn conscious of two pairs of eyes raking their backs.

"Look here." Safe out of sight in the rose garden, Mr. Wade unburdened himself. "Look here, I think we'll have to give this up. My wife looked at me just now as though she hated me."

"Don't worry," said Madeleine. "It's quite all right."

"Do you think so? I mean, I don't want to put her against me. She said several nasty things at tea."

"It's all right," said Madeleine again. "You're doing splendidly."

"Do you really think so?"

"Yes." In a lower voice she went on: "Your wife is walking round the corner of the terrace. She wants to see what we're doing. You'd better kiss me."

"Oh!" said Mr. Wade nervously. "Must I? I mean——"

"Kiss me!" said Madeleine fiercely.

Mr. Wade kissed her. Any lack of élan in the performance was remedied by Madeleine. She flung her arms round him. Mr. Wade staggered.

"Oh!" he said.

"Did you hate it very much?" said Madeleine.

"No, of course not," said Mr. Wade gallantly. "It—it just took me by surprise." He added wistfully: "Have we been in the rose garden long enough, do you think?"

"I think so," said Madeleine. "We've put in a bit of good work here."

They returned to the lawn. Mrs. Massington informed them that Mrs. Wade had gone to lie down.

Later, Mr. Wade joined Madeleine with a perturbed face.

"She's in an awful state—hysterics."

"Good."

"She saw me kissing you."

"Well, we meant her to."

"I know, but I couldn't say that, could I? I didn't know what to say. I said it had just—just—well, happened."

"Excellent."

"She said you were scheming to marry me and that you were no better than you should be. That upset me—it seemed such awfully rough luck on you. I mean, when you're just doing a job. I said that I had the utmost respect for you and that what she said wasn't true at all, and I'm afraid I got angry when she went on about it."

"Magnificent!"

"And then she told me to go away. She doesn't want ever to speak to me again. She talked of packing up and leaving." His face was dismayed.

Madeleine smiled. "I'll tell you the answer to that one. Tell her that you'll be the one to go; that you'll pack up and clear out to town."

"But I don't want to!"

"That's all right. You won't have to. Your wife would hate to think of you amusing yourself in London."

The following morning Reggie Wade had a fresh bulletin to impart.

"She says she's been thinking, and that it isn't fair for her to go away when she agreed to stay six months. But she says that as I have my friends down here she doesn't see why she shouldn't have hers. She is asking Sinclair Jordan."

"Is he *the* one?"

"Yes, and I'm damned if I'll have him in my house!"

"You must," said Madeleine. "Don't worry, I'll attend to him. Say that on thinking things over you have no objection, and that you know she won't mind your asking me to stay on, too."

"Oh, dear!" sighed Mr. Wade.

"Now don't lose heart," said Madeleine. "Everything is going splendidly. Another fortnight—and all your troubles will be over."

"A fortnight? Do you really think so?" demanded Mr. Wade.

"Think so? I'm sure of it," said Madeleine.

A week later Madeleine de Sara entered Mr. Parker Pyne's office and sank wearily into a chair.

"Enter the Queen of Vamps," said Mr. Parker Pyne, smiling.

"Vamps!" said Madeleine. She gave a hollow laugh. "I"ve never had such uphill work being a vamp. That man is obsessed by his wife! It's a disease."

Mr. Parker Pyne smiled. "Yes, indeed. Well, in one way it made our task easier. It is not every man, my dear Madeleine, whom I would expose to your fascination so lightheartedly."

The girl laughed. "If you knew the difficulty I had to make him even kiss me as though he liked it!"

"A novel experience for you, my dear. Well, is your task accomplished?"

"Yes. I think all is well. We had a tremendous scene last night. Let me see, my last report was three days ago?"

"Yes."

"Well, as I told you, I only had to look at that miserable worm, Sinclair Jordan, once. He was all over me—especially as he thought from my clothes that I had money. Mrs. Wade was furious, of course. Here were both her men dancing attendance on me. I soon showed where my preference lay. I made fun of Sinclair Jordan, to his face and to her. I laughed at his clothes, and at the length of his hair. I pointed out that he had knock knees."

"Excellent technique," said Mr. Parker Pyne appreciatively.

"Everything boiled up last night. Mrs. Wade came out in the open. She accused me of breaking up her home. Reggie Wade mentioned the little matter of Sinclair Jordan. She said that that was only the result of her unhappiness and loneliness. She had noticed her husband's abstraction for some time, but had had no idea as to the cause of it. She said they had always been ideally happy, that she adored him and he knew it, and that she wanted him and only him.

"I said it was too late for that. Mr. Wade followed his instructions splendidly. He said he didn't give a damn! He was going to marry me! Mrs. Wade could have her Sinclair as soon as she pleased. There was no reason why the divorce proceedings shouldn't be started at once; waiting six months was absurd.

"Within a few days, he said, she should have the necessary evidence and could instruct her solicitors. He said he couldn't live without me. Then Mrs. Wade clutched her chest and talked about her weak heart and had to be given brandy. He didn't weaken. He went up to town this morning, and I've no doubt she's gone after him by this time."

"So that's all right," said Mr. Pyne cheerfully. "A very satisfactory case."

The door flew open. In the doorway stood Reggie Wade.

"Is she here?" he demanded, advancing into the room. "Where is she?" He caught sight of Madeleine. "Darling!" he cried. He seized both her hands. "Darling, darling. You knew, didn't you, that it was real last night—that I meant every word I said to Iris? I don't know why I was blind so long. But I've known for the last three days."

"Known what?" said Madeleine faintly.

"That I adored you. That there was no woman in the world for me but you. Iris can bring her divorce and when it's gone through you'll marry me, won't you? Say you will, Madeleine, I adore you."

He caught the paralysed Madeleine in his arms just as the door flew open again, this time to admit a thin woman dressed in untidy green.

"I thought so!" said the newcomer. "I followed you! I knew you'd go to her!"

"I can assure you——" began Mr. Parker Pyne, recovering from the stupefaction that had descended upon him.

The intruder took no notice of him. She swept on: "Oh, Reggie, you can't want to break my heart! Only come back! I'll not say a word about all this. I'll learn golf. I won't have any friends you don't care about. After all these years, when we've been so happy together——"

"I've never been happy till now," said Mr. Wade, still gazing at Madeleine. "Dash it all, Iris, you wanted to marry that ass Jordan. Why don't you go and do it?"

Mrs. Wade gave a wail. "I hate him! I hate the very sight of him." She turned to Madeleine. "You wicked woman! You horrible vampire—stealing my husband from me."

"I don't want your husband," said Madeleine distractedly.

"Madeleine!" Mr. Wade was gazing at her in agony.

"Please go away," said Madeleine.

"But look here, I'm not pretending. I mean it."

"Oh, go away!" cried Madeleine hysterically. "Go *away*!"

Reggie moved reluctantly towards the door. "I shall come back," he warned her. "You've not seen the last of me." He went out, banging the door.

"Girls like you ought to be flogged and branded!" cried Mrs. Wade. "Reggie was an angel to me always till you came along. Now he's so changed I don't know him." With a sob, she hurried out after her husband.

Madeleine and Mr. Parker Pyne looked at each other.

"I can't help it," said Madeleine helplessly. "He's a very nice man—a dear—but I don't want to marry him. I'd no idea of all this. If you knew the difficulty I had making him kiss me!"

"Ahem!" said Mr. Parker Pyne. "I regret to admit it, but it was an error of judgment on my part." He shook his head sadly, and drawing Mr. Wade's file towards him, wrote across it:

FAILURE—owing to natural causes.
N.B.—They should have been foreseen.

THE CASE OF THE CITY CLERK

Mr. Parker Pyne leaned back thoughtfully in his swivel chair and surveyed his visitor. He saw a small sturdily built man of forty-five with wistful, puzzled, timid eyes that looked at him with a kind of anxious hopefulness.

"I saw your advertisement in the paper," said that little man nervously.

"You are in trouble, Mr. Roberts?"

"No—not in trouble exactly."

"You are unhappy?"

"I shouldn't like to say that either. I've a great deal to be thankful for."

"We all have," said Mr. Parker Pyne. "But when we have to remind ourselves of the fact it is a bad sign."

"I know," said the little man eagerly. "That's just it! You've hit the nail on the head, sir."

"Supposing you tell me all about yourself," suggested Mr. Parker Pyne.

"There's not much to tell, sir. As I say, I've a great deal to be thankful for. I have a job; I've managed to save a little money; the children are strong and healthy."

"So you want—what?"

"I—I don't know." He flushed. "I expect that sounds foolish to you, sir."

"Not at all," said Mr. Parker Pyne.

By skilled questioning he elicited further confidences. He heard of Mr. Roberts' employment in a well-known firm and of his slow but steady rise. He heard of his marriage; of the struggle to present a decent appearance, to educate the children and have them "looking nice"; of the plotting and planning and skimping and saving to put aside a few pounds each year. He heard, in fact, the saga of a life of ceaseless effort to survive.

"And—well, you see how it is," confessed Mr. Roberts. "The wife's away. Staying with her mother with the two children. Little change for them and a rest for her. No room for me and we can't afford to go elsewhere. And being alone, and reading the paper, I saw your advertisement and it set me thinking. I'm forty-eight. I just wondered. . . . Things going on everywhere," he ended, all his wistful suburban soul in his eyes.

"You want," said Mr. Pyne, "to live gloriously for ten minutes?"

"Well, I shouldn't put it like that. But perhaps you're right. Just to get out of the rut. I'd go back to it thankful afterwards—if only I had something to think about." He looked at the other man anxiously. "I suppose there's nothing possible, sir? I'm afraid—I'm afraid I couldn't afford to pay much."

"How much could you afford?"

"I could manage five pounds, sir." He waited, breathless.

"Five pounds," said Mr. Parker Pyne. "I fancy—I just fancy we might be able to manage something for five pounds. Do you object to danger?" he added sharply.

A tinge of colour came into Mr. Roberts' sallow face. "Danger, did you say, sir? Oh, no, not at all. I—I've never done anything dangerous."

Mr. Parker Pyne smiled. "Come to see me again tomorrow and I'll tell you what I can do for you."

The Bon Voyageur is a little-known hostelry. It is a restaurant frequented by a few habitués. They dislike newcomers.

To the Bon Voyageur came Mr. Pyne and was greeted with respectful recognition. "Mr. Bonnington here?" he asked.

"Yes, sir. He's at his usual table."

"Good. I'll join him."

Mr. Bonnington was a gentleman of military appearance with a somewhat bovine face. He greeted his friend with pleasure.

"Hallo, Parker. Hardly ever see you nowadays. Didn't know you came here."

"I do now and then. Especially when I want to lay my hand on an old friend."

"Meaning me?"

"Meaning you. As a matter of fact, Lucas, I've been thinking over what we were talking about the other day."

"The Peterfield business? Seen the latest in the papers? No, you can't have. It won't be in till this evening."

"What is the latest?"

"They murdered Peterfield last night," said Mr. Bonnington, placidly eating salad.

"Good heavens!" cried Mr. Pyne.

"Oh, I'm not surprised," said Mr. Bonnington. "Pigheaded old man, Peterfield. Wouldn't listen to us. Insisted on keeping the plans in his own hands."

"Did they get them?"

"No; it seems some woman came round and gave the professor a recipe for boiling a ham. The old ass, absent-minded as usual, put the recipe for the ham in his safe and the plans in the kitchen."

"Fortunate."

"Almost providential. But I still don't know who's going to take 'em to Geneva. Maitland's in the hospital. Carslake's in Berlin. I can't leave. It means young Hooper." He looked at his friend.

"You're still of the same opinion?" asked Mr. Parker Pyne.

"Absolutely. He's been got at! I know it. I haven't a shadow of proof, but I tell you, Parker, I know when a chap's crooked! And I want those plans to get to Geneva. The League needs 'em. For the first time an invention isn't going to be sold to a nation. It's going to be handed over voluntarily to the League.

"It's the finest peace gesture that's ever been attempted, and it's got to be put through. And Hooper's crooked. You'll see, he'll be drugged on the train! If he goes in a plane it'll come down at some convenient spot! But confound it all, I can't pass him over. Discipline! You've got to have discipline! That's why I spoke to you the other day."

"You asked me whether I knew of anyone."

"Yes. Thought you might in your line of business. Some fire eater spoiling for a row. Whoever *I* send stands a good chance of being done in. Your man would probably not be suspected at all. But he's got to have nerve."

"I think I know of someone who would do," said Mr. Pyne.

"Thank God there are still chaps who will take a risk. Well, it's agreed, then?"

"It's agreed," said Mr. Parker Pyne.

Mr. Parker Pyne was summing up instructions. "Now, that's quite clear? You will travel in a first-class sleeper to Geneva. You leave London at ten-forty-five, via Folkestone and Boulogne, and you get into your first-class sleeper at Boulogne. You arrive at Geneva at eight the following morning. Here is the address at which you will report. Please memorise it and I will destroy it. Afterwards go to this hotel and await further instructions. Here is sufficient money in French and Swiss notes and currency. You understand?"

"Yes, sir." Roberts' eyes were shining with excitement. "Excuse me, sir, but am I allowed to—er—know anything of what it is I am carrying?"

Mr. Parker Pyne smiled beneficently. "You are carrying a cryptogram which reveals the secret hiding-place of the crown jewels of Russia," he said solemnly. "You can understand, naturally, that Bolshevist agents will be alert to intercept you. If it is necessary for you to talk about yourself, I should recommend that you say you have come into money and are enjoying a little holiday abroad."

Mr. Roberts sipped a cup of coffee and looked out over the Lake of Geneva. He was happy but at the same time he was disappointed.

He was happy because, for the first time in his life, he was in a foreign country. Moreover, he was staying in the kind of hotel he would never stay in again, and not for one moment had he had to worry about money! He had a room with private bathroom, delicious meals and attentive service. All these things Mr. Roberts had enjoyed very much indeed.

He was disappointed because so far nothing that could be described as adventure had come his way. No disguised Bolshevists or mysterious Russians had crossed his path. A pleasant chat on the train with a French commercial traveller who spoke excellent English was the only human intercourse that had come his way. He had secreted the papers in his sponge bag as he had been told to do and had delivered them according to instructions. There had been no dangers to overcome, no hairbreadth escapes. Mr. Roberts was disappointed.

It was at that moment that a tall, bearded man murmured "*Pardon,*" and sat down on the other side of the little table. "You will excuse me," he said, "but I think you know a friend of mine. 'P.P.' are the initials."

Mr. Roberts was pleasantly thrilled. Here, at last, was a mysterious Russian. "Qu-quite right."

"Then I think we understand each other," said the stranger.

Mr. Roberts looked at him searchingly. This was far more like the real thing. The stranger was a man of about fifty, of distinguished though foreign appearance. He wore an eyeglass, and a small coloured ribbon in his button-hole.

"You have accomplished your mission in the most satisfactory manner," said the stranger. "Are you prepared to undertake a further one?"

"Certainly. Oh, yes."

"Good. You will book a sleeper on the Geneva-Paris train for to-morrow night. You will ask for Berth Number Nine."

"Supposing it is not free?"

"It will be free. That will have been seen to."

"Berth Number Nine," repeated Roberts. "Yes, I've got that."

"During the course of your journey someone will say to you, 'Pardon, Monsieur, but I think you were recently at Grasse?' To that you will reply, 'Yes, last month.' The person will then say, 'You are interested in scent?' And you will reply, 'Yes, I am a manufacturer of synthetic Oil of Jasmine.' After that you will place yourself entirely at the disposal of the person who has spoken to you. By the way, are you armed?"

"No," said little Mr. Roberts in a flutter. "No; I never thought—that is——"

"That can soon be remedied," said the bearded man. He

glanced around. No one was near them. Something hard and shining was pressed into Mr. Roberts' hand. "A small weapon but efficacious," said the stranger, smiling.

Mr. Roberts, who had never fired a revolver in his life, slipped it gingerly into a pocket. He had an uneasy feeling that it might go off at any minute.

They went over the passwords again. Then Roberts' new friend rose.

"I wish you good luck," he said. "May you come through safely. You are a brave man, Mr. Roberts."

"Am I?" thought Roberts, when the other had departed. "I'm sure I don't want to get killed. That would never do."

A pleasant thrill shot down his spine, slightly adulterated by a thrill that was not quite so pleasant.

He went to his room and examined the weapon. He was still uncertain about its mechanism and hoped he would not be called upon to use it.

He went out to book his seat.

The train left Geneva at nine-thirty. Roberts got to the station in good time. The sleeping-car conductor took his ticket and his passport, and stood aside while an underling swung Roberts' suitcase on to the rack. There was other luggage there: a pigskin case and a Gladstone bag.

"Number Nine is the lower berth," said the conductor.

As Roberts turned to leave the carriage he ran into a big man who was entering. They drew apart with apologies—Roberts' in English and the stranger's in French. He was a big burly man, with a closely shaven head and thick eye-glasses through which his eyes seemed to peer suspiciously.

"An ugly customer," said the little man to himself.

He sensed something vaguely sinister about his travelling companion. Was it to keep a watch on this man that he had been told to ask for Berth Number Nine? He fancied it might be.

He went out again into the corridor. There was still ten minutes before the train was due to start and he thought he would walk up and down the platform. Half-way along the passage he stood back to allow a lady to pass him. She was just entering the train and the conductor preceded her, ticket in hand. As she passed Roberts she dropped her handbag. The Englishman picked it up and handed it to her.

"Thank you, Monsieur." She spoke in English but her voice was foreign, a rich low voice very seductive in quality. As she was about to pass on, she hesitated and murmured: "Pardon, Monsieur, but I think you were recently at Grasse?"

Roberts' heart leaped with excitement. He was to place himself at the disposal of this lovely creature—for she *was* lovely, of that there was no doubt. Not only lovely, but aristocratic and wealthy. She wore a travelling coat of fur, a chic hat. There were pearls round her neck. She was dark and her lips were scarlet.

Roberts made the required answer. "Yes, last month."

"You are interested in scent?"

"Yes, I am a manufacturer of synthetic Oil of Jasmine."

She bent her head and passed on, leaving a mere whisper behind her. "In the corridor as soon as the train starts."

The next ten minutes seemed an age to Roberts. At last the train started. He walked slowly along the corridor. The lady in the fur coat was struggling with a window. He hurried to her assistance.

"Thank you, Monsieur. Just a little air before they insist on closing everything." And then in a soft, low, rapid voice: "After the frontier, when our fellow traveller is asleep—not before—go into the washing place and through into the compartment on the other side. You understand?"

"Yes." He let down the window and said in a louder voice: "Is that better, Madame?"

"Thank you very much."

He retired to his compartment. His travelling companion was already stretched out in the upper berth. His preparations for the night had evidently been simple. The removal of boots and a coat, in fact.

Roberts debated his own costume. Clearly, if he were going into a lady's compartment he could not undress.

He found a pair of slippers, substituted them for his boots, and then lay down, switching out the light. A few minutes later, the man above began to snore.

Just after ten o'clock they reached the frontier. The door was thrown open; a perfunctory question was asked. Had Messieurs anything to declare? The door was closed again. Presently the train drew out of Bellegarde.

The man in the upper berth was snoring again. Roberts allowed twenty minutes to elapse, then he slipped to his feet and opened the door of the lavatory compartment. Once inside, he bolted the door behind him and eyed the door on the farther side. It was not bolted. He hesitated. Should he knock?

Perhaps it would be absurd to knock. But he didn't quite like entering without knocking. He compromised, opened the door gently about an inch and waited. He even ventured on a small cough.

The response was prompt. The door was pulled open, he was seized by the arm, pulled through into the farther compartment, and the girl closed and bolted the door behind him.

Roberts caught his breath. Never had he imagined anything so lovely. She was wearing a long foamy garment of cream chiffon and lace. She leaned against the door into the corridor, panting. Roberts had often read of beautiful hunted creatures at bay. Now, for the first time, he saw one—a thrilling sight.

"Thank God!" murmured the girl.

She was quite young, Roberts noted, and her loveliness was such that she seemed to him like a being from another world. Here was romance at last—and he was in it!

She spoke in a low, hurried voice. Her English was good but the inflection was wholly foreign. "I am so glad you have come," she said. "I have been horribly frightened. Vassilievitch is on the train. You understand what that means?"

Roberts did not understand in the least what it meant, but he nodded.

"I thought I had given them the slip. I might have known better. What are we to do? Vassilievitch is in the next carriage to me. Whatever happens, he must not get the jewels. Even if he murders me, he must not get the jewels."

"He's not going to murder you and he's not going to get the jewels," said Roberts with determination.

"Then what am I to do with them?"

Roberts looked past her at the door. "The door's bolted," he said.

The girl laughed. "What are locked doors to Vassilievitch?"

Roberts felt more and more as though he were in the middle of one of his favourite novels. "There's only one thing to be done. Give them to me."

She looked at him doubtfully. "They are worth a quarter of a million."

Roberts flushed. "You can trust me."

The girl hesitated a moment longer, then: "Yes, I will trust you," she said. She made a swift movement. The next minute she was holding out to him a rolled-up pair of stockings—stockings of cobweb silk. "Take them, my friend," she said to the astonished Roberts.

He took them and at once he understood. Instead of being light as air, the stockings were unexpectedly heavy.

"Take them into your compartment," she said. "You can give them to me in the morning—if—if I am still here."

Roberts coughed. "Look here," he said. "About you." He paused. "I—I must keep guard over you." Then he flushed in an agony of propriety. "Not in here, I mean. I'll stay in there." He nodded towards the lavatory compartment.

"If you like to stay here——" She glanced at the upper unoccupied berth.

Roberts flushed to the roots of his hair. "No, no," he protested. "I shall be all right in there. If you need me, call out."

"Thank you, my friend," said the girl softly.

She slipped into the lower berth, drew up the covers and smiled at him gratefully. He retreated into the wash-room.

Suddenly—it must have been a couple of hours later—he thought he heard something. He listened—nothing. Perhaps he had been mistaken. And yet it certainly seemed to him that he had heard a faint sound from the next carriage. Supposing—just supposing . . .

He opened the door softly. The compartment was as he had left it, with the tiny blue light in the ceiling. He stood there with his eyes straining through the dimness till they got accustomed to it. He made out the outline of the berth.

He saw that it was empty. The girl was not there!

He switched the light full on. The compartment was empty. Suddenly he sniffed. Just a whiff but he recognised it—the sweet, sickly odour of chloroform!

He stepped from the compartment (unlocked now, he

noted) out into the corridor and looked up and down it. Empty! His eyes fastened on the door next to the girl's. She had said that Vassilievitch was in the next compartment. Gingerly Roberts tried the handle. The door was bolted on the inside.

What should he do? Demand admittance? But the man would refuse—and after all, the girl might not be there! And if she were, would she thank him for making a public business of the matter? He had gathered that secrecy was essential in the game they were playing.

A perturbed little man wandered slowly along the corridor. He paused at the end compartment. The door was open, and the conductor lay there sleeping. And above him, on a hook, *hung his brown uniform coat and peaked cap.*

In a flash Roberts had decided on his course of action. In another minute he had donned the coat and cap, and was hurrying back along the corridor. He stopped at the door next to that of the girl, summoned all his resolution and knocked peremptorily.

When the summons was not answered, he knocked again.

"Monsieur," he said, in his best accent.

The door opened a little way and a head peered out—the head of a foreigner, clean-shaven except for a black moustache. It was an angry, malevolent face.

"*Qu'est-ce-qu'il y a?*" he snapped.

"*Votre passeport, monsieur.*" Roberts stepped back and beckoned.

The other hesitated, then stepped out into the corridor. Roberts had counted on his doing that. If he had the girl inside, he naturally would not want the conductor to come in. Like a flash, Roberts acted. With all his force he shoved the foreigner aside—the man was unprepared and the swaying of the train helped—bolted into the carriage himself, shut the door and locked it.

Lying across the end of the berth was the girl, a gag across her mouth and her wrists tied together. He freed her quickly, and she fell against him with a sigh.

"I feel so weak and ill," she murumred. "It was chloroform, I think. Did he—did he get them?"

"No." Roberts tapped his pocket. "What are we to do now?" he asked.

The girl sat up. Her wits were returning. She took in his costume.

"How clever of you. Fancy thinking of that! He said he would kill me if I did not tell him where the jewels were. I have been so afraid—and then you came." Suddenly she laughed. "But we have outwitted him! He will not dare do anything. He cannot even try to get back into his own compartment.

"We must stay here till morning. Probably he will leave the train at Dijon; we are due to stop there in about half an hour. He will telegraph to Paris and they will pick up our trail there. In the meantime, you had better throw that coat and cap out of the window. They might get you into trouble."

Roberts obeyed.

"We must not sleep," the girl decided. "We must stay on guard till morning."

It was a strange, exciting vigil. At six o'clock in the morning, Roberts opened the door carefully and looked out. No one was about. The girl slipped quickly into her own compartment. Roberts followed her in. The place had clearly been ransacked. He regained his own carriage through the wash-room. His fellow-traveller was still snoring.

They reached Paris at seven o'clock. The conductor was declaiming at the loss of his coat and cap. He had not yet discovered the loss of a passenger.

Then began a most entertaining chase. The girl and Roberts took taxi after taxi across Paris. They entered hotels and restaurants by one door and left them by another. At last the girl gave a sigh.

"I feel sure we are not followed now," she said. "We have shaken them off."

They breakfasted and drove to Le Bourget. Three hours later they were at Croydon. Roberts had never flown before.

At Croydon a tall old gentleman with a far-off resemblance to Mr. Roberts' mentor at Geneva was waiting for them. He greeted the girl with especial respect.

"The car is here, madam," he said.

"This gentleman will accompany us, Paul," said the girl. And to Roberts: "Count Paul Stepanyi."

The car was a vast limousine. They drove for about an hour, then they entered the grounds of a country house and pulled up at the door of an imposing mansion. Mr. Roberts was taken to a room furnished as a study. There he handed over the precious pair of stockings. He was left alone for a while. Presently Count Stepanyi returned.

"Mr. Roberts," he said, "our thanks and gratitude are due to you. You have proved yourself a brave and resourceful man." He held out a red morocco case. "Permit me to confer upon you the Order of St. Stanislaus—tenth class with laurels."

As in a dream Roberts opened the case and looked at the jewelled order. The old gentleman was still speaking.

"The Grand Duchess Olga would like to thank you herself before you depart."

He was led to a big drawing-room. There, very beautiful in a flowing robe, stood his travelling companion.

She made an imperious gesture of the hand, and the other man left them.

"I owe you my life, Mr. Roberts," said the grand duchess.

She held out her hand. Roberts kissed it. She leaned suddenly towards him.

"You are a brave man," she said.

His lips met hers; a waft of rich Oriental perfume surrounded him.

For a moment he held that slender, beautiful form in his arms. . . .

He was still in a dream when somebody said to him: "The car will take you anywhere you wish."

An hour later, the car came back for the Grand Duchess Olga. She got into it and so did the white-haired man. He had removed his beard for coolness. The car set down the Grand Duchess Olga at a house in Streatham. She entered it and an elderly woman looked up from a tea table.

"Ah, Maggie, dear, so there you are."

In the Geneva-Paris express this girl was the Grand Duchess Olga; in Mr. Parker Pyne's office she was Madeleine de Sara, and in the house at Streatham she was Maggie

Sayers, fourth daughter of an honest, hard-working family.
How are the mighty fallen!

Mr. Parker Pyne was lunching with his friend. "Congratulations," said the latter, "your man carried the thing through without a hitch. The Tormali gang must be wild to think the plans of that gun have gone to the League. Did you tell your man what it was he was carrying?"

"No. I thought it better to—er—embroider."

"Very discreet of you."

"It wasn't exactly discretion. I wanted him to enjoy himself. I fancied he might find a gun a little tame. I wanted him to have some adventures."

"Tame?" said Mr. Bonnington, staring at him. "Why, that lot would murder him as soon as look at him."

"Yes," said Mr. Parker Pyne mildly. "But I didn't want him to be murdered."

"Do you make a lot of money in your business, Parker?" asked Mr. Bonnington.

"Sometimes I lose it," said Mr. Parker Pyne. "That is, if it is a deserving case."

Three angry gentlemen were abusing one another in Paris.

"That confounded Hooper!" said one. "He let us down."

"The plans were not taken by anyone from the office," said the second. "But they went Wednesday, I am assured of that. And so I say *you* bungled it."

"I didn't," said the third sulkily; "there was no Englishman on the train except a little clerk. He'd never heard of Peterfield or of the gun. I know. I tested him. Peterfield and the gun meant nothing to him." He laughed. "He had a Bolshevist complex of some kind."

Mr. Roberts was sitting in front of a gas fire. On his knee was a letter from Mr. Parker Pyne. It enclosed a cheque for fifty pounds "from certain people who are delighted with the way a certain commission was executed."

On the arm of his chair was a library book. Mr. Roberts opened it at random. "She crouched against the door like a beautiful hunted creature at bay."

Well, he knew all about that.

He read another sentence: "He sniffed the air. The faint, sickly odour of chloroform came to his nostrils."

That he knew about too.

"He caught her in his arms and felt the responsive quiver of her scarlet lips."

Mr. Roberts gave a sigh. It wasn't a dream. It had all happened. The journey out had been dull enough, but the journey home! He had enjoyed it. But he was glad to be home again. He felt vaguely that life could not be lived indefinitely at such a pace. Even the Grand Duchess Olga—even that last kiss—partook already of the unreal quality of a dream.

Mary and the children would be home to-morrow. Mr. Roberts smiled happily.

She would say: "We've had such a nice holiday. I hated thinking of you all alone here, poor old boy." And he'd say: "That's all right, old girl. I had to go to Geneva for the firm on business—delicate bit of negotiations—and look what they've sent me." And he'd show her the cheque for fifty pounds.

He thought of the Order of St. Stanislaus, tenth class with laurels. He'd hidden it, but supposing Mary found it! It would take a bit of explaining. . . .

Ah, that was it—he'd tell her he'd picked it up abroad. A curio.

He opened his book again and read happily. No longer was there a wistful expression on his face.

He, too, was of that glorious company to whom Things Happened.

THE CASE OF THE RICH WOMAN

The name of Mrs. Abner Rymer was brought to Mr. Parker Pyne. He knew the name and he raised his eyebrows.

Presently his client was shown into the room.

Mrs. Rymer was a tall woman, big-boned. Her figure was ungainly and the velvet dress and the heavy fur coat she wore did not disguise the fact. The knuckles of her large hands were pronounced. Her face was big and broad and highly coloured. Her black hair was fashionably dressed, and there were many tips of curled ostrich in her hat.

She plumped herself down on a chair with a nod. "Good-morning," she said. Her voice had a rough accent. "If you're any good at all you'll tell me how to spend my money!"

"Most original," murmured Mr. Parker Pyne. "Few ask that in these days. So you really find it difficult, Mrs. Rymer?"

"Yes, I do," said the lady bluntly. "I've got three fur coats, a lot of Paris dresses and such like. I've got a car and a house in Park Lane. I've had a yacht, but I don't like the sea. I've got a lot of those high-class servants that look down their nose at you. I've travelled a bit and seen foreign parts. And I'm blessed if I can think of anything more to buy or do." She looked hopefully at Mr. Pyne.

"There are hospitals," he said.

"What? Give it away, you mean? No, that I won't do! That money was worked for, let me tell you, worked for hard. If you think I'm going to hand it out like so much dirt—well, you're mistaken. I want to spend it; spend it and get some good out of it. Now, if you've got any ideas that are worth while in that line, you can depend on a good fee."

"Your proposition interests me," said Mr. Pyne. "You do not mention a country house."

"I forgot it, but I've got one. Bores me to death."

"You must tell me more about yourself. Your problem is not easy to solve."

"I'll tell you and willing. I'm not ashamed of what I've come from. Worked in a farmhouse, I did, when I was a girl. Hard work it was too. Then I took up with Abner—he was a workman in the mills near by. He courted me for eight years, and then we got married."

"And you were happy?" asked Mr. Pyne.

"I was. He was a good man to me, Abner. We had a hard struggle of it, though; he was out of a job twice, and children coming along. Four we had, three boys and a girl. And none of them lived to grow up. I dare say it would have been different if they had." Her face softened; looked suddenly younger.

"His chest was weak—Abner's was. They wouldn't take him for the war. He did well at home. He was made foreman. He was a clever fellow, Abner. He worked out a process. They treated him fair, I will say; gave him a good sum for it. He used that money for another idea of his. That brought in money hand over fist. He was a master now, employing his own workmen. He bought two concerns that were bankrupt and made them pay. The rest was easy. Money came in hand over fist. It's still coming in.

"Mind you, it was rare fun at first. Having a house and a tip-top bathroom and servants of one's own. No more cooking and scrubbing and washing to do. Just sit back on your silk cushions in the drawing-room and ring the bell for tea—like any countess might! Grand fun it was, and we enjoyed it. And then we came up to London. I went to swell dressmakers for my clothes. We went to Paris and the Riviera. Rare fun it was."

"And then?" said Mr. Parker Pyne.

"We got used to it, I suppose," said Mrs. Rymer. "After a bit it didn't seem so much fun. Why, there were days when we didn't even fancy our meals properly—us, with any dish we fancied to choose from! As for baths—well, in the end, one bath a day's enough for anyone. And Abner's health began to worry him. Paid good money to doctors, we did, but they couldn't do anything. They tried this and they tried that. But it was no use. He died." She paused. "He was a young man, only forty-three."

Mr. Pyne nodded sympathetically.

"That was five years ago. Money's still rolling in. It seems wasteful not to be able to do anything with it. But as I tell you, I can't think of anything else to buy that I haven't got already."

"In other words," said Mr. Pyne, "your life is dull. You are not enjoying it."

"I'm sick of it," said Mrs. Rymer gloomily. "I've no friends. The new lot only want subscriptions, and they laugh at me behind my back. The old lot won't have anything to do with me. My rolling up in a car makes them shy. Can you do anything, or suggest anything?"

"It is possible that I can," said Mr. Pyne slowly. "It will be difficult, but I believe there is a chance of success. I think it's possible I can give you back what you have lost—your interest in life."

"How?" demanded Mrs. Rymer curtly.

"That," said Mr. Parker Pyne, "is my professional secret. I never disclose my methods beforehand. The question is, will you take a chance? I do not guarantee success, but I do think there is a reasonable possibility of it."

"And how much will it cost?"

"I shall have to adopt unusual methods, and therefore it will be expensive. My charges will be one thousand pounds, payable in advance."

"You can open your mouth all right, can't you?" said Mrs. Rymer appreciatively. "Well, I'll risk it. I'm used to paying top price. Only, when I pay for a thing, I take good care that I get it."

"You shall get it," said Mr. Parker Pyne. "Never fear."

"I'll send you the cheque this evening," said Mrs. Rymer, rising. "I'm sure I don't know why I should trust you. Fools and their money are soon parted, they say. I dare say I'm a fool. You've got nerve, to advertise in all the papers that you can make people happy!"

"Those advertisements cost me money," said Mr. Pyne. "If I could not make my words good, that money would be wasted. I *know* what causes unhappiness, and consequently I have a clear idea of how to produce an opposite condition."

Mrs. Rymer shook her head doubtfully and departed, leaving a cloud of expensive mixed essences behind her.

The handsome Claude Luttrell strolled into the office. "Something in my line?"

Mr. Pyne shook his head. "Nothing so simple," he said. "No, this is a difficult case. We must, I fear, take a few risks. We must attempt the unusual."

"Mrs. Oliver?"

Mr. Pyne smiled at the mention of the world-famous novelist. "Mrs. Oliver," he said, "is really the most conventional of all of us. I have in mind a bold and audacious coup. By the way, you might ring up Doctor Antrobus."

"Antrobus?"

"Yes. His services will be needed."

A week later Mrs. Rymer once more entered Mr. Parker Pyne's office. He rose to receive her.

"This delay, I assure you, has been necessary," he said.

"Many things had to be arranged, and I had to secure the services of an unusual man who had to come half-across Europe."

"Oh!" She said it suspiciously. It was constantly present in her mind that she had paid out a cheque for a thousand pounds and the cheque had been cashed.

Mr. Parker Pyne touched a buzzer. A young girl, dark, Oriental looking, but dressed in white nurse's kit, answered it.

"Is everything ready, Nurse de Sara?"

"Yes. Doctor Constantine is waiting."

"What are you going to do?" asked Mrs. Rymer, with a touch of uneasiness.

"Introduce you to some Eastern magic, dear lady," said Mr. Parker Pyne.

Mrs. Rymer followed the nurse up to the next floor. Here she was ushered into a room that bore no relation to the rest of the house. Oriental embroideries covered the walls. There were divans with soft cushions and beautiful rugs on the floor. A man was bending over a coffee-pot. He straightened as they entered.

"Doctor Constantine," said the nurse.

The doctor was dressed in European clothes, but his face was swarthy and his eyes were dark and oblique with a peculiarly piercing power in their glance.

"So this is my patient?" he said in a low, vibrant voice.

"I'm not a patient," said Mrs. Rymer.

"Your body is not sick," said the doctor, "but your soul is weary. We of the East know how to cure that disease. Sit down and drink a cup of coffee."

Mrs. Rymer sat down and accepted a tiny cup of the fragrant brew. As she sipped it the doctor talked.

"Here in the West, they treat only the body. A mistake. The body is only the instrument. A tune is played upon it. It may be a sad, weary tune. It may be a gay tune full of delight. That last is what we shall give you. You have money. You shall spend it and enjoy. Life shall be worth living again. It is easy—easy—so easy . . ."

A feeling of languor crept over Mrs. Rymer. The figures of the doctor and the nurse grew hazy. She felt blissfully happy and very sleepy. The doctor's figure grew bigger. The whole world was growing bigger.

The doctor was looking into her eyes. "Sleep," he was saying. "Sleep. Your eyelids are closing. Soon you will sleep. You will sleep. You will sleep . . ."

Mrs. Rymer's eyelids closed. She floated with a wonderful great big world. . . .

When her eyes opened it seemed to her that a long time had passed. She remembered several things vaguely—strange, impossible dreams; then a feeling of waking; then further dreams. She remembered something about a car and the dark, beautiful girl in nurse's uniform bending over her.

Anyway, she was properly awake now, and in her own bed.

At least, was it her own bed? It felt different. It lacked the delicious softness of her own bed. It was vaguely reminiscent of days almost forgotten. She moved, and it creaked. Mrs. Rymer's bed in Park Lane never creaked.

She looked round. Decidedly, this was not Park Lane. Was it a hospital? No, she decided, not a hospital. Nor was it a hotel. It was a bare room, the walls an uncertain shade of lilac. There was a deal wash-stand with a jug and basin upon it. There was a deal chest of drawers and a tin trunk. There were unfamiliar clothes hanging on pegs. There was the bed covered with a much-mended quilt and there was herself in it.

"Where *am* I?" said Mrs. Rymer.

The door opened and a plump little woman bustled in. She had red cheeks and a good-humoured air. Her sleeves were rolled up and she wore an apron.

"There!" she exclaimed. "She's awake. Come in, doctor."

Mrs. Rymer opened her mouth to say several things—but they remained unsaid, for the man who followed the plump woman into the room was not in the least like the elegant, swarthy Doctor Constantine. He was a bent old man who peered through thick glasses.

"That's better," he said, advancing to the bed and taking up Mrs. Rymer's wrist. "You'll soon be better now, my dear."

"What's been the matter with me?" demanded Mrs. Rymer.

"You had a kind of seizure," said the doctor. "You've been unconscious for a day or two. Nothing to worry about."

"Gave us a fright, you did, Hannah," said the plump woman. "You've been raving too, saying the oddest things."

"Yes, yes, Mrs. Gardner," said the doctor repressively. "But we mustn't excite the patient. You'll soon be up and about again, my dear."

"But don't you worry about the work, Hannah," said Mrs. Gardner. "Mrs. Roberts has been in to give me a hand and we've got on fine. Just lie still and get well, my dear."

"Why do you call me Hannah?" said Mrs. Rymer.

"Well, it's your name," said Mrs. Gardner, bewildered.

"No, it isn't. My name is Amelia. Amelia Rymer. Mrs. Abner Rymer."

The doctor and Mrs. Gardner exchanged glances.

"Well, just you lie still," said Mrs. Gardner.

"Yes, yes; no worry," said the doctor.

They withdrew. Mrs. Rymer lay puzzling. Why did they call her Hannah, and why had they exchanged that glance of amused incredulity when she had given them her name? Where was she, and what had happened?

She slipped out of bed. She felt a little uncertain on her legs, but she walked slowly to the small dormer window and looked out—on a farmyard! Completely mystified, she went back to bed. What was she doing in a farmhouse that she had never seen before?

Mrs. Gardner re-entered the room with a bowl of soup on a tray.

Mrs. Rymer began her questions. "What am I doing in this house?" she demanded. "Who brought me here?"

"Nobody brought you, my dear. It's your home. Leastways, you've lived here for the last five years—and me not suspecting once that you were liable to fits."

"*Lived* here! *Five* years?"

"That's right. Why, Hannah, you don't mean that you still don't remember?"

"I've never lived here! I've never seen you before."

"You see, you've had this illness and you've forgotten."

"I've never lived here."

"But you have, my dear." Suddenly Mrs. Gardner darted across to the chest of drawers and brought to Mrs. Rymer a faded photograph in a frame.

It represented a group of four persons: a bearded man, a plump woman (Mrs. Gardner), a tall, lank man with a pleasantly sheepish grin, and somebody in a print dress and apron—herself!

Stupefied, Mrs. Rymer gazed at the photograph. Mrs. Gardner put the soup down beside her and quietly left the room.

Mrs. Rymer sipped the soup mechanically. It was good soup, strong and hot. All the time her brain was in a whirl. Who was mad? Mrs. Gardner or herself? One of them must be! But there was the doctor too.

"I'm Amelia Rymer," she said firmly to herself. "I know I'm Amelia Rymer and nobody's going to tell me different."

She had finished the soup. She put the bowl back on the tray. A folded newspaper caught her eye and she picked it up and looked at the date on it, October 19. What day had she gone to Mr. Parker Pyne's office? Either the fifteenth or the sixteenth. Then she must have been ill for three days.

"That rascally doctor!" said Mrs. Rymer wrathfully.

All the same, she was a shade relieved. She had heard of cases where people had forgotten who they were for years at a time. She had been afraid some such thing had happened to her.

She began turning the pages of the paper, scanning the columns idly, when suddenly a paragraph caught her eye.

Mrs. Abner Rymer, widow of Abner Rymer, the "button shank" king, was removed yesterday to a private home for mental cases. For the past two days she has persisted in declaring she was not herself, but a servant girl named Hannah Moorhouse.

"Hannah Moorhouse! So that's it," said Mrs. Rymer. "She's me, and I'm her. Kind of double, I suppose. Well, we can soon put *that* right! If that oily hypocrite of a Parker Pyne is up to some game or other——"

But at this minute her eye was caught by the name

Constantine staring at her from the printed page. This time it was a headline.

DR. CONSTANTINE'S CLAIM

At a farewell lecture given last night on the eve of his departure for Japan, Dr. Claudius Constantine advanced some startling theories. He declared that it was possible to prove the existence of the soul by transferring a soul from one body to another. In the course of his experiments in the East he had, he claimed, successfully effected a double transfer—the soul of a hypnotised body A being transferred to a hypnotised body B and the soul of B to the body of A. On recovering from the hypnotic sleep, A declared herself to be B, and B thought herself to be A. For the experiment to succeed, it was necessary to find two people with a great bodily resemblence. It was an undoubted fact that two people resembling each other were *en rapport*. This was very noticeable in the case of twins, but two strangers, varying widely in social position, but with a marked similarity of feature, were found to exhibit the same harmony of structure.

Mrs. Rymer cast the paper from her. "The scoundrel! The black scoundrel!"

She saw the whole thing now! It was a dastardly plot to get hold of her money. This Hannah Moorhouse was Mr. Pyne's tool—possibly an innocent one. He and that devil Constantine had brought off this fantastic coup.

But she'd expose him! She'd show him up! She'd have the law on him! She'd tell everyone——

Abruptly Mrs. Rymer came to a stop in the tide of her indignation. She remembered that first paragraph. Hannah Moorhouse had not been a docile tool. She had protested; had declared her individuality. And what had happened?

"Clapped into a lunatic asylum, poor girl," said Mrs. Rymer.

A chill ran down her spine.

A lunatic asylum. They got you in there and they never let you get out. The more you said you were sane, the less they'd believe you. There you were and there you stayed. No, Mrs. Rymer wasn't going to run the risk of that.

The door opened and Mrs. Gardner came in.

"Ah, you've drunk your soup, my dear. That's good. You'll soon be better now."

"When was I taken ill?" demanded Mrs. Rymer.

"Let me see. It was three days ago—on Wednesday. That was the fifteenth. You were took bad about four o'clock."

"Ah!" The ejaculation was fraught with meaning. It had been just about four o'clock when Mrs. Rymer had entered the presence of Doctor Constantine.

"You slipped down in your chair," said Mrs. Gardner. "'Oh!' you says. 'Oh!' just like that. And then: 'I'm falling asleep,' you says in a dreamy voice. 'I'm falling asleep.' And fall asleep you did, and we put you to bed and sent for the doctor, and here you've been ever since."

"I suppose," Mrs. Rymer ventured, "there isn't any way you could know who I am—apart from my face, I mean."

"Well, that's a queer thing to say," said Mrs. Gardner. "What is there to go by better than a person's face, I'd like to know? There's your birthmark, though, if that satisfies you better."

"A birthmark?" said Mrs. Rymer, brightening. She had no such thing.

"Strawberry mark just under the right elbow," said Mrs. Gardner. "Look for yourself, my dear."

"This will prove it," said Mrs. Rymer to herself. She knew that she had no strawberry mark under the right elbow. She turned back the sleeve of her nightdress. The strawberry mark was there.

Mrs. Rymer burst into tears.

Four days later, Mrs. Rymer rose from her bed. She had thought out several plans of action and rejected them.

She might show the paragraph in the paper to Mrs. Gardner and the doctor and explain. Would they believe her? Mrs. Rymer was sure they would not.

She might go to the police. Would they believe her? Again she thought not.

She might go to Mr. Pyne's office. That idea undoubtedly pleased her best. For one thing, she would like to tell that oily scoundrel what she thought of him. She was debarred from putting this plan into operation by a vital obstacle. She was at present in Cornwall (so she had learned), and she had no money for the journey to London. Two and fourpence in a worn purse seemed to represent her financial position.

And so, after four days, Mrs. Rymer made a sporting decision. For the present she would accept things! She was Hannah Moorhouse. Very well, she would be Hannah Moorhouse. For the present she would accept that rôle, and later, when she had saved sufficient money, she would go to London and beard the swindler in his den.

And having thus decided, Mrs. Rymer accepted her rôle with perfect good temper, even with a kind of sardonic amusement. History was repeating itself indeed. This life here reminded her of her girlhood. How long ago that seemed!

The work was a bit hard after her years of soft living, but after the first week she found herself slipping into the ways of the farm.

Mrs. Gardner was a good-tempered, kindly woman. Her husband, a big, taciturn man, was kindly also. The lank, shambling man of the photograph had gone; another farmhand came in his stead, a good-humoured giant of forty-five, slow of speech and thought, but with a shy twinkle in his blue eyes.

The weeks went by. At last the day came when Mrs. Rymer had enough money to pay her fare to London. But she did not go. She put it off. Time enough, she thought. She wasn't easy in her mind about asylums yet. That scoundrel, Parker Pyne, was clever. He'd get a doctor to say she was mad and she'd be clapped away out of sight with no one knowing anything about it.

"Besides," said Mrs. Rymer to herself, "a bit of a change does one good."

She rose early and worked hard. Joe Welsh, the new farmhand, was ill that winter, and she and Mrs. Gardner nursed him. The big man was pathetically dependent on them.

Spring came—lambing time; there were wild flowers in

the hedges, a treacherous softness in the air. Joe Welsh gave Hannah a hand with her work. Hannah did Joe's mending.

Sometimes, on Sundays, they went for a walk together. Joe was a widower. His wife had died four years before. Since her death he had, he frankly confessed it, taken a drop too much.

He didn't go much to the Crown nowadays. He bought himself some new clothes. Mr. and Mrs. Gardner laughed.

Hannah made fun of Joe. She teased him about his clumsiness. Joe didn't mind. He looked bashful but happy.

After spring came summer—a good summer that year. Everyone worked hard.

Harvest was over. The leaves were red and golden on the trees.

It was October eighth when Hannah looked up one day from a cabbage she was cutting and saw Mr. Parker Pyne leaning over the fence.

"You!" said Hannah, alias Mrs. Rymer. "You . . ."

It was some time before she got it all out, and when she had said her say, she was out of breath.

Mr. Parker Pyne smiled blandly. "I quite agree with you," he said.

"A cheat and a liar, that's what you are!" said Mrs. Rymer, repeating herself. "You with your Constantines and your hypnotising, and that poor girl Hannah Moorhouse shut up with—loonies."

"No," said Mr. Parker Pyne, "there you misjudge me. Hannah Moorhouse is not in a lunatic asylum, because Hannah Moorhouse never existed."

"Indeed?" said Mrs. Rymer. "And what about the photograph of her that I saw with my own eyes?"

"Faked," said Mr. Pyne. "Quite a simple thing to manage."

"And the piece in the paper about her?"

"The whole paper was faked so as to include two items in a natural manner which would carry conviction. As it did."

"That rogue, Doctor Constantine!"

"An assumed name—assumed by a friend of mine with a talent for acting."

Mrs. Rymer snorted. "Ho! And I wasn't hypnotised either, I suppose?"

"As a matter of fact, you were not. You drank in your coffee a preparation of Indian hemp. After that, other drugs were administered and you were brought down here by car and allowed to recover consciousness."

"Then Mrs. Gardner has been in it all the time?" said Mrs. Rymer.

Mr. Parker Pyne nodded.

"Bribed by you, I suppose! Or filled up with a lot of lies!"

"Mrs. Gardner trusts me," said Mr. Pyne. "I once saved her only son from penal servitude."

Something in his manner silenced Mrs. Rymer on that tack. "What about the birthmark!" she demanded.

Mr. Pyne smiled. "It is already fading. In another six months it will have disappeared altogether."

"And what's the meaning of all this tomfoolery? Making a fool of me, sticking me down here as a servant—me with all that good money in the bank. But I suppose I needn't ask. You've been helping yourself to it, my fine fellow. That's the meaning of all this."

"It is true," said Mr. Parker Pyne, "that I did obtain from you, while you were under the influence of drugs, a power of attorney and that during your—er—absence, I have assumed control of your financial affairs, but I can assure you, my dear madam, that apart from that original thousand pounds, no money of yours has found its way into my pocket. As a matter of fact, by judicious investments your financial position is actually improved." He beamed at her.

"Then why——?" began Mrs. Rymer.

"I am going to ask you a question, Mrs. Rymer," said Mr. Pyne. "You are an honest woman. You will answer me honestly, I know. I am going to ask you if you are happy."

"Happy! That's a pretty question! Steal a woman's money and ask her if she's happy. I like your impudence!"

"You are still angry," he said. "Most natural. But leave my misdeeds out of it for the moment. Mrs. Rymer, when you came to my office a year ago to-day, you were an unhappy woman. Will you tell me that you are unhappy now? If so, I apologise, and you are at liberty to take what steps you please against me. Moreover, I will refund you the thousand pounds you paid me. Come, Mrs. Rymer, are you an unhappy woman now?"

Mrs. Rymer looked at Mr. Parker Pyne, but she dropped her eyes when she spoke at last.

"No," she said. "I'm not unhappy." A tone of wonder crept into her voice. "You've got me there. I admit it. I've not been as happy as I am now since Abner died. I—I'm going to marry a man who works here—Joe Welsh. Our banns are going up next Sunday; that is, they *were* going up next Sunday."

"But now, of course," said Mr. Pyne, "everything is different."

Mrs. Rymer's face flamed. She took a step forward.

"What do you mean—different? Do you think if I had all the money in the world it would make me a lady? I don't want to be a lady, thank you; a helpless, good-for-nothing lot they are. Joe's good enough for me and I'm good enough for him. We suit each other and we're going to be happy. As for you, Mr. Nosey Parker, you take yourself off and don't interfere with what doesn't concern you!"

Mr. Parker Pyne took a paper from his pocket and handed it to her. "The power of attorney," he said. "Shall I tear it up? You will assume control of your own fortune now, I take it."

A strange expression came over Mrs. Rymer's face. She thrust back the paper.

"Take it. I've said hard things to you—and some of them you deserved. You're a downy fellow, but all the same I trust you. Seven hundred pounds I'll have in the bank here—that'll buy us a farm we've got our eye on. The rest of it—well, let the hospitals have it."

"You cannot mean to hand over your entire fortune to hospitals?"

"That's just what I do mean. Joe's a dear, good fellow, but he's weak. Give him money and you'd ruin him. I've got him off the drink now, and I'll keep him off it. Thank God, I know my own mind. I'm not going to let money come between me and happiness."

"You are a remarkable woman," said Mr. Pyne slowly. "Only one woman in a thousand would act as you are doing."

"Then only one woman in a thousand's got sense," said Mrs. Rymer.

"I take off my hat to you," said Mr. Parker Pyne, and there was an unusual note in his voice. He raised his hat with solemnity and moved away.

"And Joe's never to know, mind!" Mrs. Rymer called after him.

She stood there with the dying sun behind her, a great blue-green cabbage in her hands, her head thrown back and her shoulders squared. A grand figure of a peasant woman, outlined against the setting sun. . . .

HAVE YOU GOT EVERYTHING YOU WANT?

"*Par ici, Madame.*"

A tall woman in a mink coat followed her heavily encumbered porter along the platform of the Gare de Lyon.

She wore a dark-brown knitted hat pulled down over one eye and ear. The other side revealed a charming tip-tilted profile and little golden curls clustering over a shell-like ear. Typically an American, she was altogether a very charming-looking creature and more than one man turned to look at her as she walked past the high carriages of the waiting train.

Large plates were stuck in holders on the sides of the carriages.

PARIS—ATHENES. PARIS—BUCHAREST. PARIS—STAMBOUL

At the last named the porter came to an abrupt halt. He undid the strap which held the suit-cases together and they slipped heavily to the ground. "*Voici, Madame.*"

The *wagon-lit* conductor was standing beside the steps. He came forward, remarking, "*Bonsoir, Madame,*" with an empressement perhaps due to the richness and perfection of the mink coat.

The woman handed him her sleeping-car ticket of flimsy paper.

"Number Six," he said; "this way."

He sprang nimbly into the train, the woman following him. As she hurried down the corridor after him, she nearly collided with a portly gentleman who was emerging from the compartment next to hers. She had a momentary glimpse of a large bland face with benevolent eyes.

"*Voici, Madame.*"

The conductor displayed the compartment. He threw up the window and signalled to the porter. A lesser employee took in the baggage and put it up in the racks. The woman sat down.

Beside her on the seat she had placed a small scarlet case and her handbag. The carriage was hot, but it did not seem to occur to her to take off her coat. She stared out of the window with unseeing eyes. People were hurrying up and down the platform. There were sellers of newspapers, of pillows, of chocolate, of fruit, of mineral waters. They held up their wares to her, but her eyes looked blankly through them. The Gare de Lyon had faded from her sight. On her face were sadness and anxiety.

"If Madame will give me her passport?"

The words made no impression on her. The conductor, standing in the doorway, repeated them. Elsie Jeffries roused herself with a start.

"I beg your pardon?"

"Your passport, Madame."

She opened her bag, took out the passport and gave it to him.

"That will be all right, Madame, I will attend to everything." A slight significant pause. "I shall be going with Madame as far as Stamboul."

Elsie drew out a fifty-franc note and handed it to him. He accepted it in a business-like manner, and inquired when she would like her bed made up and whether she was taking dinner.

These matters settled, he withdrew and almost immediately the restaurant man came rushing down the corridor ringing his little bell frantically, and bawling out, "*Premier service. Premier service.*"

Elsie rose, divested herself of the heavy fur coat, took a brief glance at herself in the little mirror, and picking up her handbag and jewel case, stepped out into the corridor. She had gone only a few steps when the restaurant man came rushing along on his return journey. To avoid him, Elsie stepped back for a moment into the doorway of the adjoining compartment, which was now empty. As the man passed and she prepared to continue her journey to the dining-car, her glance fell idly on the label of a suit-case which was lying on the seat.

It was a stout pigskin case, somewhat worn. On the label were the words, "J. Parker Pyne, passenger to Stamboul." The suit-case itself bore the initials "P.P."

A startled expression came over the girl's face. She hesitated a moment in the corridor, then going back to her own compartment she picked up a copy of *The Times* which she had laid down on the table with some magazines and books.

She ran her eye down the advertisement columns on the front page, but what she was looking for was not there. A slight frown on her face, she made her way to the restaurant car.

The attendant allotted her a seat at a small table already tenanted by one person—the man with whom she had nearly collided in the corridor. In fact, the owner of the pigskin suit-case.

Elsie looked at him without appearing to do so. He seemed very bland, very benevolent, and in some way impossible to explain, delightfully reassuring. He behaved in reserved British fashion, and it was not till the fruit was on the table that he spoke.

"They keep these places terribly hot," he said.

"I know," said Elsie. "I wish one could have the window open."

He gave a rueful smile. "Impossible! Every person present except ourselves would protest."

She gave an answering smile. Neither said any more.

Coffee was brought and the usual indecipherable bill. Having laid some notes upon it, Elsie suddenly took her courage in both hands.

"Excuse me," she murmured. "I saw your name upon your suit-case—Parker Pyne. Are you—are you, by any chance——?"

She hesitated and he came quickly to her rescue.

"I believe I am. That is"—he quoted from the advertisement which Elsie had noticed more than once in *The Times,* and for which she had searched vainly just now: "'Are you happy? If not, consult Mr. Parker Pyne.' Yes, I'm that one, all right."

"I see," said Elsie. "How—how extraordinary!"

He shook his head. "Not really. Extraordinary from your point of view, but not from mine." He smiled reassuringly, then leaned forward. Most of the other diners had left the car. "So you are unhappy?" he said.

"I——" began Elsie, and stopped.

"You would not have said 'How extraordinary' otherwise," he pointed out.

Elsie was silent a minute. She felt strangely soothed by the mere presence of Mr. Parker Pyne. "Ye-es," she admitted at last. "I am—unhappy. At least, I am worried."

He nodded sympathetically.

"You see," she continued, "a very curious thing has happened—and I don't know in the least what to make of it."

"Suppose you tell me about it," suggested Mr. Pyne.

Elsie thought of the advertisement. She and Edward had often commented on it and laughed. She had never thought that she . . . perhaps she had better not. . . . If Mr. Parker Pyne were a charlatan. . . . But he looked—nice!

Elsie made her decision. Anything to get this worry off her mind.

"I'll tell you. I'm going to Constantinople to join my husband. He does a lot of Oriental business, and this year he found it necessary to go there. He went a fortnight ago. He was to get things ready for me to join him. I've been very excited at the thought of it. You see, I've never been abroad before. We've been in England six months."

"You and your husband are both American?"

"Yes."

"And you have not, perhaps, been married very long?"

"We've been married a year and a half."

"Happily?"

"Oh, yes! Edward's a perfect angel." She hesitated. "Not, perhaps, very much go to him. Just a little—well, I'd call it straightlaced. Lot of puritan ancestry and all that. But he's a *dear,*" she added hastily.

Mr. Parker Pyne looked at her thoughtfully for a moment or two, then he said, "Go on."

"It was about a week after Edward had started. I was writing a letter in his study, and I noticed that the blotting paper was all new and clean, except for a few lines of writing across it. I'd just been reading a detective story with a clue in a blotter and so, just for fun, I held it up to a mirror. It really *was* just fun, Mr. Pyne—I mean, I wasn't spying on Edward or anything like that. I mean, he's such a mild lamb one wouldn't dream of anything of that kind."

"Yes, yes; I quite understand."

"The thing was quite easy to read. First there was the word 'wife,' then 'Simplon Express,' and lower down, 'just before Venice would be the best time.'" She stopped.

"Curious," said Mr. Pyne. "Distinctly curious. It was your husband's handwriting?"

"Oh, yes. But I've cudgelled my brains and I cannot see under what circumstances he would write a letter with just those words in it."

"'Just before Venice would be the best time,'" repeated Mr. Parker Pyne. "Distinctly curious."

Mrs. Jeffries was leaning forward looking at him with a flattering hopefulness. "What shall I do?" she asked simply.

"I am afraid," said Mr. Parker Pyne, "that we shall have to wait until before Venice." He took up a folder from the table. "Here is the schedule time of our train. It arrives at Venice at two-twenty-seven to-morrow afternoon."

They looked at each other.

"Leave it to me," said Parker Pyne.

It was five minutes past two. The Simplon Express was eleven minutes late. It had passed Mestre about a quarter of an hour before.

Mr. Parker Pyne was sitting with Mrs. Jeffries in her compartment. So far the journey had been pleasant and uneventful. But now the moment had arrived when, if anything was going to happen, it presumably would happen. Mr. Parker Pyne and Elsie faced each other. Her heart was beating fast, and her eyes sought his in a kind of anguished appeal for reassurance.

"Keep perfectly calm," he said. "You are quite safe. I am here."

Suddenly a scream broke out from the corridor.

"Oh, look—look! The train is on fire!"

With a bound Elsie and Mr. Parker Pyne were in the corridor. An agitated woman with a Slav countenance was pointing a dramatic finger. Out of one of the front compartments smoke was pouring in a cloud. Mr. Parker Pyne and Elsie ran along the corridor. Others joined them. The compartment in question was full of smoke. The first comers drew back, coughing. The conductor appeared.

"The compartment is empty!" he cried. "Do not alarm yourselves, *messieurs et dames*. *Le feu*, it will be controlled."

A dozen excited questions and answers broke out. The train was running over the bridge that joins Venice to the mainland.

Suddenly Mr. Parker Pyne turned, forced his way through the little pack of people behind him and hurried down the corridor to Elsie's compartment. The lady with the Slav face was seated in it, drawing deep breaths from the open window.

"Excuse me, Madame," said Parker Pyne. "But this is not your compartment."

"I know. I know," said the Slav lady. "*Pardon*. It is the shock, the emotion—my heart." She sank back on the seat and indicated the open window. She drew her breath in great gasps.

Mr. Parker Pyne stood in the doorway. His voice was fatherly and reassuring. "You must not be afraid," he said. "I do not think for a moment that the fire is serious."

"Not? Ah, what a mercy! I feel restored." She half-rose. "I will return to my own compartment."

"Not just yet." Mr. Parker Pyne's hand pressed her gently back. "I will ask of you to wait a moment, Madame."

"Monsieur, this is an outrage!"

"Madame, you will remain."

His voice rang out coldly. The woman sat still looking at him. Elsie joined them.

"It seems it was a smoke bomb," she said breathlessly. "Some ridiculous practical joke. The conductor is furious.

He is asking everybody——" She broke off, staring at the second occupant of the carriage.

"Mrs. Jeffries," said Mr. Parker Pyne, "what do you carry in your little scarlet case?"

"My jewellery."

"Perhaps you would be so kind as to look and see that everything is there."

There was immediately a torrent of words from the Slav lady. She broke into French, the better to do justice to her feelings.

In the meantime Elsie had picked up the jewel case. "Oh!" she cried. "It's unlocked."

"*. . . Et je porterai plainte à la Compagnie des Wagons-Lits,*" finished the Slav lady.

"They're gone!" cried Elsie. "Everything! My diamond bracelet. And the necklace Pop gave me. And the emerald and ruby rings. And some lovely diamond brooches. Thank goodness I was wearing my pearls. Oh, Mr. Pyne, what shall we do?"

"If you will fetch the conductor," said Mr. Parker Pyne, "I will see that this woman does not leave this compartment till he comes."

"*Scélérat! Monstre!*" shrieked the Slav lady. She went on to further insults. The train drew in to Venice.

The events of the next half-hour may be briefly summarised. Mr. Parker Pyne dealt with several different officials in several different languages—and suffered defeat. The suspected lady consented to be searched—and emerged without a stain on her character. The jewels were not on her.

Between Venice and Trieste Mr. Parker Pyne and Elsie discussed the case.

"When was the last time you actually saw your jewels?"

"This morning. I put away some sapphire ear-rings I was wearing yesterday and took out a pair of plain pearl ones."

"And all the jewellery was there intact?"

"Well, I didn't go through it all, naturally. But it looked the same as usual. A ring or something like that might have been missing, but not more."

Mr. Parker Pyne nodded. "Now, when the conductor made up the compartment this morning?"

"I had the case with me—in the restaurant car. I always take it with me. I've never left it except when I ran out just now."

"Therefore," said Mr. Parker Pyne, "that injured innocent, Madame Subayska, or whatever she calls herself, *must* have been the thief. But what the devil did she do with the things? She was only in here a minute and a half—just time to open the case with a duplicate key and take out the stuff—yes, but what next?"

"Could she have handed them to anyone else?"

"Hardly. I had turned back and was forcing my way along the corridor. If anyone had come out of this compartment I should have seen them."

"Perhaps she threw them out of the window to someone."

"An excellent suggestion; only, as it happens, we were passing over the sea at that moment. We were on the bridge."

"Then she must have hidden them actually in the carriage."

"Let's hunt for them."

With true transatlantic energy Elsie began to look about. Mr. Parker Pyne participated in the search in a somewhat absent fashion. Reproached for not trying, he excused himself.

"I'm thinking that I must send a rather important telegram at Trieste," he explained.

Elsie received the explanation coldly. Mr. Parker Pyne had fallen heavily in her estimation.

"I'm afraid you're annoyed with me, Mrs. Jeffries," he said meekly.

"Well, you've not been very successful," she retorted.

"But, my dear lady, you must remember I am not a detective. Theft and crime are not in my line at all. The human heart is my province."

"Well, I was a bit unhappy when I got on this train," said Elsie, "but nothing to what I am now! I could just cry buckets. My lovely, lovely bracelet—and the emerald ring Edward gave me when we were engaged."

"But surely you are insured against theft?" Mr. Parker Pyne interpolated.

"Am I? I don't know. Yes, I suppose I am. But it's the *sentiment* of the thing, Mr. Pyne."

The train slackened speed. Mr. Parker Pyne peered out of the window. "Trieste," he said. "I must send my telegram."

"Edward!" Elsie's face lighted up as she saw her husband hurrying to meet her on the platform at Stamboul. For the moment even the loss of her jewellery faded from her mind. She forgot the curious words she had found on the blotter. She forgot everything except that it was a fortnight since she had seen her husband last, and that in spite of being sober and straightlaced he was really a most attractive person.

They were just leaving the station when Elsie felt a friendly tap on the shoulder and turned to see Mr. Parker Pyne. His bland face was beaming good-naturedly.

"Mrs. Jeffries," he said, "will you come to see me at the Hotel Tokatlian in half an hour? I think I may have some good news for you."

Elsie looked uncertainly at Edward. Then she made the introduction. "This—er—is my husband—Mr. Parker Pyne."

"As I believe your wife wired you, her jewels have been stolen," said Mr. Parker Pyne. "I have been doing what I can to help her recover them. I think I may have news for her in about half an hour."

Elsie looked inquiringly at Edward. He replied promptly:

"You'd better go, dear. The Tokatlian, you said, Mr. Pyne? Right; I'll see she makes it."

It was just half an hour later that Elsie was shown into Mr. Parker Pyne's private sitting-room. He rose to receive her.

"You've been disappointed in me, Mrs. Jeffries," he said. "Now, don't deny it. Well, I don't pretend to be a magician, but I do what I can. Take a look inside here."

He passed along the table a small stout cardboard box. Elsie opened it. Rings, brooches, bracelet, necklace—they were all there.

"Mr. Pyne, how marvellous! How—how too wonderful!"

Mr. Parker Pyne smiled modestly. "I am glad not to have failed you, my dear young lady."

"Oh, Mr. Pyne, you make me feel just mean! Ever since Trieste I've been horrid to you. And now—this. But how did you get hold of them? When? Where?"

Mr. Parker Pyne shook his head thoughtfully. "It's a long story," he said. "You may hear it one day. In fact, you may hear it quite soon."

"Why can't I hear it now?"

"There are reasons," said Mr. Parker Pyne.

And Elsie had to depart with her curiosity unsatisfied.

When she had gone, Mr. Parker Pyne took up his hat and stick and went out into the streets of Pera. He walked along smiling to himself, coming at last to a little café, deserted at the moment, which overlooked the Golden Horn. On the other side, the mosques of Stamboul showed slender minarets against the afternoon sky. It was very beautiful. Mr. Pyne sat down and ordered two coffees. They came thick and sweet. He had just begun to sip his when a man slipped into the seat opposite. It was Edward Jeffries.

"I have ordered some coffee for you," said Mr. Parker Pyne, indicating the little cup.

Edward pushed the coffee aside. He leaned forward across the table. "How did you know?" he asked.

Mr. Parker Pyne sipped his coffee dreamily. "Your wife will have told you about her discovery on the blotter? No? Oh, but she will tell you; it has slipped her mind for the moment."

He mentioned Elsie's discovery.

"Very well; that linked up perfectly with the curious incident that happened just before Venice. For some reason or other you were engineering the theft of your wife's jewels. But why the phrase 'just before Venice would be the best time'? There seemed nonsense in that. Why did you not leave it to your—agent—to choose her own time and place?

"And then, suddenly, I saw the point. *Your wife's jewels were stolen before you yourself left London and were replaced by paste duplicates.* But that solution did not satisfy you. You were a high-minded, conscientious young man. You have a horror of some servant or other innocent person being suspected. A theft must actually occur—at a place and in a manner which will leave no suspicion attached to anybody of your acquaintance or household.

"Your accomplice is provided with a key to the jewel box and a smoke bomb. At the correct moment she gives the alarm, darts into your wife's compartment, unlocks the jewel case and flings the paste duplicates into the sea. She may be suspected and searched, but nothing can be proved against her, since the jewels are not in her possession.

"And now the significance of the place chosen becomes apparent. If the jewels had merely been thrown out by the side of the line, they might have been found. Hence the importance of the one moment when the train is passing over the sea.

"In the meantime, you make your arrangements for selling the jewellery here. You have only to hand over the stones when the robbery has actually taken place. My wire, however, reached you in time. You obeyed my instructions and deposited the box of jewellery at the Tokatlian to await my arrival, knowing that otherwise I should keep my threat of placing the matter in the hands of the police. You also obeyed my instructions in joining me here."

Edward Jeffries looked at Mr. Parker Pyne appealingly. He was a good-looking young man, tall and fair, with a round chin and very round eyes. "How can I make you understand?" he said hopelessly. "To you I must seem just a common thief."

"Not at all," said Mr. Parker Pyne. "On the contrary, I should say you are almost painfully honest. I am accustomed to the classification of types. You, my dear sir, fall naturally into the category of victims. Now, tell me the whole story."

"I can tell you that in one word—blackmail."

"Yes?"

"You've seen my wife; you realise what a pure, innocent creature she is—without thought or knowledge of evil."

"Yes, yes."

"She has the most marvellously pure ideals. If she were to find out about—about anything I had done, she would leave me."

"I wonder. But that is not the point. What *have* you done, my young friend? I presume this is some affair with a woman?"

Edward Jeffries nodded.

"Since your marriage—or before?"

"Before—oh, before."

"Well, well, what happened?"

"Nothing; nothing at all. This is just the cruel part of it.

It was at a hotel in the West Indies. There was a very attractive woman—a Mrs. Rossiter—staying there. Her husband was a violent man; he had the most savage fits of temper. One night he threatened her with a revolver. She escaped from him and came to my room. She was half-crazy with terror. She—she asked me to let her stay there till morning. I—what else could I do?"

Mr. Parker Pyne gazed at the young man, and the young man gazed back with conscious rectitude. Mr. Parker Pyne sighed. "In other words, to put it plainly, you were had for a mug, Mr. Jeffries."

"Really——"

"Yes, yes. A very old trick—but it often comes off successfully with quixotic young men. I suppose, when your approaching marriage was announced, the screw was turned?"

"Yes. I received a letter. If I did not send a certain sum of money, everything would be disclosed to my prospective father-in-law. How I had—had alienated this young woman's affection from her husband; how she had been seen coming to my room. The husband would bring a suit for divorce. Really, Mr. Pyne, the whole thing made me out the most utter blackguard." He wiped his brow in a harassed manner.

"Yes, yes, I know. And so you paid. And from time to time the screw has been put on again."

"Yes. This was the last straw. Our business has been badly hit by the slump. I simply could not lay my hands on any ready money. I hit upon this plan." He picked up his cup of cold coffee, looked at it absently, and drank it. "What am I to do now?" he demanded pathetically. "What *am* I to do, Mr. Pyne?"

"You will be guided by me," said Parker Pyne firmly. "I will deal with your tormentors. As to your wife, you will go straight back to her and tell her the truth—or at least a portion of it. The only point where you will deviate from the truth is concerning the actual facts in the West Indies. You must conceal from her the fact that you were—well, had for a mug, as I said before."

"But——"

"My dear Mr. Jeffries, you do not understand women. If a woman has to choose between a mug and a Don Juan, she will choose Don Juan every time. Your wife, Mr. Jeffries, is a charming, innocent, high-minded girl, and the only way she is going to get any kick out of her life with you is to believe that she has reformed a rake."

Edward Jeffries was staring at him open-mouthed.

"I mean what I say," said Mr. Parker Pyne. "At the present moment your wife is in love with you, but I see signs that she may not remain so if you continue to present to her a picture of such goodness and rectitude that it is almost synonymous with dullness."

Edward winced.

"Go to her, my boy," said Mr. Parker Pyne kindly. "Confess everything—that is, as many things as you can think of. Then explain that from the moment you met her you gave up all this life. You even stole so that it might not come to her ears. She will forgive you enthusiastically."

"But when there's nothing really to forgive——"

"What is truth?" said Mr. Parker Pyne. "In my experience it is usually the thing that upsets the apple cart! It is a fundamental axiom of married life that you *must* lie to a woman. She likes it! Go and be forgiven, my boy. And live happily ever afterwards. I dare say your wife will keep a wary eye on you in future whenever a pretty woman comes along—some men would mind that, but I don't think you will."

"I never want to look at any woman but Elsie," said Mr. Jeffries simply.

"Splendid, my boy," said Mr. Parker Pyne. "But I shouldn't let her know that if I were you. No woman likes to feel she's taken on too soft a job."

Edward Jeffries rose. "You really think——?"

"I *know*," said Mr. Parker Pyne, with force.

THE GATE OF BAGHDAD

"Four great gates has the city of Damascus. . . ."

Mr. Parker Pyne repeated Flecker's lines softly to himself.

"Postern of Fate, the Desert Gate, Disaster's Cavern, Fort of Fear,

The Portal of Bagdad am I, the Doorway of Diarbekir."

He was standing in the streets of Damascus and drawn up outside the Oriental Hotel he saw one of the huge six-wheeled Pullmans that was to transport him and eleven other people across the desert to Baghdad on the morrow.

"Pass not beneath, O Caravan, or pass not singing. Have you heard
That silence where the birds are dead yet something pipeth like a bird?
Pass out beneath, O Caravan, Doom's Caravan, Death's Caravan!"

Something of a contrast now. Formerly the Gate of Baghdad *had* been the gate of Death. Four hundred miles of desert to traverse by caravan. Long weary months of travel. Now the ubiquitous petrol-fed monsters did the journey in thirty-six hours.

"What were you saying, Mr. Parker Pyne?"

It was the eager voice of Miss Netta Pryce, youngest and most charming of the tourist race. Though encumbered by a stern aunt with the suspicion of a beard and a thirst for Biblical knowledge, Netta managed to enjoy herself in many frivolous ways of which the elder Miss Pryce might possibly have not approved.

Mr. Parker Pyne repeated Flecker's lines to her.

"How thrilling," said Netta.

Three men in Air Force uniform were standing near and one of them, an admirer of Netta's, struck in.

"There are still thrills to be got out of the journey," he said. "Even nowadays the convoy is occasionally shot up by bandits. Then there's losing yourself—that happens sometimes. And we are sent out to find you. One fellow was lost for five days in the desert. Luckily he had plenty of water with him. Then there are the bumps. Some bumps! One man was killed. It's the truth I'm telling you! He was asleep and his head struck the top of the car and it killed him."

"In the six-wheeler, Mr. O'Rourke?" demanded the elder Miss Pryce.

"No—not in the six-wheeler," admitted the young man.

"But we must do some sight-seeing," cried Netta.

Her aunt drew out a guide book.

Netta edged away.

"I know she'll want to go to some place where St. Paul was lowered out of a window," she whispered. "And I do so want to see the bazaars."

O'Rourke responded promptly.

"Come with me. We'll start down the Street called Straight——"

They drifted off.

Mr. Parker Pyne turned to a quiet man standing beside him, Hensley by name. He belonged to the public works department of Baghdad.

"Damascus is a little disappointing when one sees it for the first time," he said apologetically. "A little civilised. Trams and modern houses and shops."

Hensley nodded. He was a man of few words.

"Not got—back of beyond—when you think you have," he jerked out.

Another man drifted up, a fair young man wearing an old Etonian tie. He had an amiable but slightly vacant face which at the moment looked worried. He and Hensley were in the same department.

"Hallo, Smethurst," said his friend. "Lost anything?"

Captain Smethurst shook his head. He was a young man of somewhat slow intellect.

"Just looking round," he said vageuly. Then he seemed to rouse himself. "Ought to have a beano to-night. What?"

The two friends went off together. Mr. Parker Pyne bought a local paper printed in French.

He did not find it very interesting. The local news meant nothing to him and nothing of importance seemed to be going on elsewhere. He found a few paragraphs headed *Londres*.

The first referred to financial matters. The second dealt with the supposed destination of Mr. Samuel Long, the defaulting financier. His defalcations now amounted to the sum of three millions and it was rumoured that he had reached South America.

"Not too bad for a man just turned thirty," said Mr. Parker Pyne to himself.

"I beg your pardon?"

Parker Pyne turned to confront an Italian General who

had been on the same boat with him from Brindisi to Beirut.

Mr. Parker Pyne explained his remark. The Italian General nodded his head several times.

"He is a great criminal, that man. Even in Italy we have suffered. He inspired confidence all over the world. He is a man of breeding, too, they say."

"Well, he went to Eton and Oxford," said Mr. Parker Pyne cautiously.

"Will he be caught, do you think?"

"Depends on how much of a start he got. He may be still in England. He may be—anywhere."

"Here with us?" the General laughed.

"Possibly." Mr. Parker Pyne remained serious. "For all you know, General, *I* may be he."

The General gave him a startled glance. Then his olive-brown face relaxed into a smile of comprehension.

"Oh! that is very good—very good indeed. But you——"

His eyes strayed downwards from Mr. Parker Pyne's face.

Mr. Parker Pyne interpreted the glance correctly.

"You mustn't judge by appearances," he said. "A little additional—er—*embonpoint*—is easily managed and has a remarkably ageing effect."

He added dreamily:

"Then there is hair dye, of course, and face stain, and even a change of nationality."

General Poli withdrew doubtfully. He never knew how far the English were serious.

Mr. Parker Pyne amused himself that evening by going to a cinema. Afterwards he was directed to a "Nightly Palace of Gaieties." It appeared to him to be neither a palace nor gay. Various ladies danced with a distinct lack of *verve*. The applause was languid.

Suddenly Mr Parker Pyne caught sight of Smethurst. The young man was sitting at a table alone. His face was flushed and it occurred to Mr. Parker Pyne that he had already drunk more than was good for him. He went across and joined the young man.

"Disgraceful, the way these girls treat you," said Captain Smethurst gloomily. "Bought her two drinks—three drinks

—lots of drinks. Then she goes off laughing with some dago. Call it a disgrace."

Mr. Parker Pyne sympathised. He suggested coffee.

"Got some araq coming," said Smethurst. "Jolly good stuff. You try it."

Mr. Parker Pyne knew something of the properties of araq. He employed tact. Smethurst, however, shook his head.

"I'm in a bit of a mess," he said. "Got to cheer myself up. Don't know what you'd do in my place. Don't like to go back on a pal, what? I mean to say—and yet—what's a fellow to do?"

He studied Mr. Parker Pyne as though noticing him for the first time.

"Who are you?" he demanded with the curtness born of his potations. "What do you do?"

"The confidence trick," said Mr. Parker Pyne gently.

Smethurst gazed at him in lively concern.

"What—you too?"

Mr. Parker Pyne drew from his wallet a cutting. He laid it on the table in front of Smethurst.

"*Are you unhappy?* (So it ran.) *If so, consult Mr. Parker Pyne.*"

Smethurst focused it after some difficulty.

"Well, I'm damned," he ejaculated. "You meantersay—people come and tell you things?"

"They confide in me—yes."

"Pack of idiotic women, I suppose."

"A good many women," admitted Mr. Parker Pyne. "But men also. What about you, my young friend? You wanted advice just now?"

"Shut your damned head," said Captain Smethurst. "No business of anybody's—anybody's 'cept mine. Where's that goddamned araq?"

Mr. Parker Pyne shook his head sadly.

He gave up Captain Smethurst as a bad job.

The convoy for Baghdad started at seven o'clock in the morning. There was a party of twelve. Mr. Parker Pyne and General Poli, Miss Pryce and her niece, three Air Force officers, Smethurst and Hensley and an Armenian mother and son by name Pentemian.

The journey started uneventfully. The fruit trees of Damascus were soon left behind. The sky was cloudy and the young driver looked at it doubtfully once or twice. He exchanged remarks with Hensley.

"Been raining a good bit the other side of Rutbah. Hope we shan't stick."

They made a halt at midday and square cardboard boxes of lunch were handed round. The two drivers brewed tea which was served in cardboard cups. They drove on again across the flat interminable plain.

Mr. Parker Pyne thought of the slow caravans and the weeks of journeying. . . .

Just at sunset they came to the desert fort of Rutbah.

The great gates were unbarred and the six-wheeler drove in through them into the inner courtyard of the fort.

"This feels exciting," said Netta.

After a wash she was eager for a short walk. Flight-Lieutenant O'Rourke and Mr. Parker Pyne offered themselves as escorts. As they started the manager came up to them and begged them not to go far away as it might be difficult to find their way back after dark.

"We'll only go a short way," O'Rourke promised.

Walking was not, indeed, very interesting owing to the sameness of the surroundings.

Once Mr. Parker Pyne bent and picked something up.

"What is it?" asked Netta curiously.

He held it out to her.

"A prehistoric flint, Miss Pryce—a borer."

"Did they—kill each other with them?"

"No—it had a more peaceful use. But I expect they could have killed with it if they'd wanted to. It's the *wish* to kill that counts—the mere instrument doesn't matter. *Something* can always be found."

It was getting dark, and they ran back to tho fort.

After a dinner of many courses of the tinned variety they sat and smoked. At twelve o'clock the six-wheeler was to proceed.

The driver looked anxious.

"Some bad patches near here," he said. "We may stick."

They all climbed into the big car and settled themselves.

Miss Pryce was annoyed not to be able to get at one of her suit-cases.

"I should like my bedroom slippers," she said.

"More likely to need your gum boots," said Smethurst. "If I know the look of things we'll be stuck in a sea of mud."

"I haven't even got a change of stockings," said Netta.

"That's all right. You'll stay put. Only the stronger sex has to get out and heave."

"Always carry spare socks," said Hensley, patting his overcoat pocket. "Never know."

The lights were turned out. The big car started out into the night.

The going was not too good. They were not jolted as they would have been in a touring car, but nevertheless they got a bad bump now and then.

Mr. Parker Pyne had one of the front seats. Across the aisle was the Armenian lady shrouded in wraps and shawls. Her son was behind her. Behind Mr. Parker Pyne were the two Miss Pryces. The General, Smethurst, Hensley and the R.A.F. men were at the back.

The car rushed on through the night. Mr. Parker Pyne found it hard to sleep. His position was cramped. The Armenian lady's feet stuck out and encroached on his preserve. She, at any rate, was comfortable.

Everyone else seemed to be asleep. Mr. Parker Pyne felt drowsiness stealing over him, when a sudden jolt threw him up towards the roof of the car. He heard a drowsy protest from the back of the six-wheeler. "Steady. Want to break our necks?"

Then the drowsiness returned. A few minutes later, his neck sagging uncomfortably. Mr. Parker Pyne slept. . . .

He was awakened suddenly. The six-wheeler had stopped. Some of the men were getting out. Hensley spoke briefly.

"We're stuck."

Anxious to see all there was to see, Mr. Parker Pyne stepped gingerly out in the mud. It was not raining now. Indeed there was a moon and by its light the drivers could be seen frantically at work with jacks and stones, striving to raise the wheels. Most of the men were helping. From the windows of the six-wheeler the three women looked out,

Miss Pryce and Netta with interest, the Armenian lady with ill-concealed disgust.

At a command from the driver, the male passengers obediently heaved.

"Where's that Armenian fellow?" demanded O'Rourke. "Keeping his toes warmed and comfortable like a cat? Let's have him out too."

"Captain Smethurst too," observed General Poli. "He is not with us."

"The blighter's asleep still. Look at him."

True enough, Smethurst still sat in his arm-chair, his head sagging forward and his whole body slumped down.

"I'll rouse him," said O'Rourke.

He sprang in through the door. A minute later he reappeared. His voice had changed.

"I say. I think he's ill—or something. Where's the doctor?"

Squadron Leader Loftus, the Air Force doctor, a quiet-looking man with greying hair, detached himself from the group by the wheel.

"What's the matter with him?" he asked.

"I—don't know."

The doctor entered the car. O'Rourke and Parker Pyne followed him. He bent over the sagging figure. One look and touch was enough.

"He's dead," he said quietly.

"Dead? But how?" Questions shot out. "Oh! how dreadful!" from Netta.

Loftus looked round in an irritated manner.

"Must have hit his head against the top," he said. "We went over one bad bump."

"Surely that wouldn't kill him? Isn't there anything else?"

"I can't tell unless I examine him properly," snapped Loftus. He looked round him with a harassed air. The women were pressing closer. The men outside were beginning to crowd in.

Mr. Parker Pyne spoke to the driver. He was a strong athletic young man. He lifted each female passenger in turn, carrying her across the mud and setting her down on dry land. Madame Pentemian and Netta he managed easily, but he staggered under the weight of the hefty Miss Pryce.

The interior of the six-wheeler was left clear for the doctor to make his examination.

The men went back to their efforts to jack up the car. Presently the sun rose over the horizon. It was a glorious day. The mud was drying rapidly, but the car was still stuck. Three jacks had been broken and so far no efforts had been of any avail. The drivers started preparing breakfast—opening tins of sausages and boiling water for tea.

A little way apart Squadron Leader Loftus was giving his verdict.

"There's no mark or wound on him. As I said, he must have hit his head against the top."

"You're satisfied he died naturally?" asked Mr. Parker Pyne.

There was something in his voice that made the doctor look at him quickly.

"There's only one other possibility."

"Yes."

"Well, that someone hit him on the back of the head with something in the nature of a sandbag." His voice sounded apologetic.

"That's not very likely," said Williamson, the other Air Force officer. He was a cherubic-looking youth. "I mean, nobody could do that without our seeing."

"If we were asleep?" suggested the doctor.

"Fellow couldn't be sure of that," pointed out the other. "Getting up and all that would have roused someone or other."

"The only way," said General Poli, "would be for anyone sitting behind him. He could choose his moment and need not even rise from his seat."

"Who was sitting behind Captain Smethurst?" asked the doctor.

O'Rourke replied readily.

"Hensley, sir—so that's no good. Hensley was Smethurst's best pal."

There was a silence. Then Mr. Parker Pyne's voice rose with quiet certainty.

"I think," he said, "that Flight Lieutenant Williamson has something to tell us."

"I, sir? I—well——"

"Out with it, Williamson," said O'Rourke.

"It's nothing, really—nothing at all."

"Out with it."

"It's only a scrap of conversation I overheard—at Rutbah—in the courtyard. I'd got back into the six-wheeler to look for my cigarette case. I was hunting about. Two fellows were just outside talking. One of them was Smethurst. He was saying——"

He paused.

"Come on, man, out with it."

"Something about not wanting to let a pal down. He sounded very distressed. Then he said: 'I'll hold my tongue till Baghdad—but not a minute afterwards. You'll have to get out quickly.'"

"And the other man?"

"I don't know, sir. I swear I don't. It was dark and he only said a word or two and that I couldn't catch."

"Who amongst you knows Smethurst well?"

"I don't think the words—a pal—could refer to anyone but Hensley," said O'Rourke slowly. "I knew Smethurst, but very slightly. Williamson is new out—so is Squadron Leader Loftus. I don't think either of them have ever met him before."

Both men agreed.

"You, General?"

"I never saw the young man until we crossed the Lebanon in the same car from Beirut."

"And that Armenian rat?"

"He couldn't be a pal," said O'Rourke with decision. "And no Armenian would have the nerve to kill anyone."

"I have, perhaps, a small additional piece of evidence," said Mr. Parker Pyne.

He repeated the conversation he had had with Smethurst in the café at Damascus.

"He made use of the phrase—'don't like to go back on a pal,'" said O'Rourke thoughtfully. "And he was worried."

"Has no one else anything to add?" asked Mr. Parker Pyne.

The doctor coughed.

"It may have nothing to do with it——" he began.

He was encouraged.

"It was just that I heard Smethurst say to Hensley, 'You can't deny that there is a leakage in your department.'"

"When was this?"

"Just before starting from Damascus yesterday morning. I thought they were just talking shop. I didn't imagine——" He stopped.

"My friends, this is interesting," said the General. "Piece by piece you assemble the evidence."

"You said a sandbag, doctor," said Mr. Parker Pyne. "Could a man manufacture such a weapon?"

"Plenty of sand," said the doctor dryly. He took some up in his hand as he spoke.

"If you put some in a sock," began O'Rourke and hesitated.

Everyone remembered two short sentences spoken by Hensley the night before.

"*Always carry spare socks. Never know.*"

There was silence. Then Mr. Parker Pyne said quietly, "Squadron Leader Loftus, I believe Mr. Hensley's spare socks are in the pocket of his overcoat which is now in the car."

Their eyes went for one minute to where a moody figure was pacing to and from on the horizon. Hensley had held aloof since the discovery of the dead man. His wish for solitude had been respected since it was known that he and the dead man had been friends.

Mr. Parker Pyne went on:

"Will you get them and bring them here?"

The doctor hesitated.

"I don't like——" he muttered. He looked again at that pacing figure. "Seems a bit low down——"

"You must get them, please," said Mr. Parker Pyne. "The circumstances are unusual. We are marooned here. And we have got to know the truth. If you will fetch those socks I fancy we shall be a step nearer."

Loftus turned away obediently.

Mr. Parker Pyne drew General Poli a little aside.

"General, I think it was you who sat across the aisle from Captain Smethurst."

"That is so."

"Did anyone get up and pass down the car?"

"Only the English lady, Miss Pryce. She went to the wash place at the back."

"Did she stumble at all?"

"She lurched a little with the movement of the car, naturally."

"She was the only person you saw moving about?"

"Yes."

The General looked at him curiously and said, "Who are you, I wonder? You take command, yet you are not a soldier."

"I have seen a good deal of life," said Mr. Parker Pyne.

"You have travelled, eh?"

"No," said Mr. Parker Pyne. "I have sat in an office."

Loftus returned carrying the socks. Mr. Parker Pyne took them from him and examined them. *To the inside of one of them wet sand still adhered.*

Mr. Parker Pyne drew a deep breath.

"Now I know," he said.

All their eyes went to the pacing figure on the horizon.

"I should like to look at the body if I may," said Mr. Parker Pyne.

He went with the doctor to where Smethurst's body had been laid down covered with a tarpaulin.

The doctor removed the cover.

"There's nothing to see," he said.

But Mr. Parker Pyne's eyes were fixed on the dead man's tie.

"So Smethurst was an old Etonian," he said.

Loftus looked surprised.

Then Mr. Parker Pyne surprised him still further.

"What do you know of young Williamson?" he asked.

"Nothing at all. I only met him at Beirut. I'd come from Egypt. But why? Surely——"

"Well, it's on his evidence we're going to hang a man, isn't it?" said Mr. Parker Pyne cheerfully. "One's got to be careful."

He still seemed to be interested in the dead man's tie and collar. He unfastened the studs and removed the collar. Then he uttered an exclamation.

"See that?"

On the back of the collar was a small round bloodstain.

He peered closer down at the uncovered neck.

"This man wasn't killed by a blow on the head, doctor," he said briskly. "He was stabbed—at the base of the skull. You can just see the tiny puncture."

"And I missed it!"

"You'd got your preconceived notion," said Mr. Parker Pyne apologetically. "A blow on the head. It's easy enough to miss this. You can hardly see the wound. A quick stab with a small sharp instrument and death would be instantaneous. The victim wouldn't even cry out."

"Do you mean a stiletto? You think the General——?"

"Italians and stilettos go together in the popular fancy —— Hallo, here comes a car!"

A touring car had appeared over the horizon.

"Good," said O'Rourke as he came up to join them. "The ladies can go on in that."

"What about our murderer?" asked Mr. Parker Pyne.

"You mean Hensley——?"

"No, I don't mean Hensley," said Mr. Parker Pyne. "I happen to know that Hensley's innocent."

"You—but why?"

"Well, you see, he had sand in his sock."

O'Rourke stared.

"I know, my boy," said Mr. Parker Pyne gently, "it doesn't sound like sense, but it is. Smethurst wasn't hit on the head, you see, he was stabbed."

He paused a minute and then went on.

"Just cast your mind back to the conversation I told you about—the conversation we had in the café. You picked out what was, to you, the significant phrase. But it was another phrase that struck me. When I said to him that I did the Confidence Trick he said '*What, you too?*' Doesn't that strike you as rather curious? I don't know that you'd describe a series of peculations from a Department as a 'Confidence Trick.' Confidence Trick is more descriptive of someone like the absconding Mr. Samuel Long, for instance."

The doctor started. O'Rourke said: "Yes—perhaps . . ."

"I said in jest that perhaps the absconding Mr. Long was one of our party. Suppose that that is the truth."

"What—but it's impossible!"

"Not at all. What do you know of people besides their

passports and the accounts they give of themselves. Am I really Mr. Parker Pyne? Is General Poli really an Italian General? And what of the masculine Miss Pryce senior who needs a shave most distinctly."

"But he—but Smethurst—didn't know Long?"

"Smethurst is an old Etonian. Long also, was at Eton. Smethurst may have known him although he didn't tell you so. He may have recognised him amongst us. And if so, what is he to do? He has a simple mind, and he worries over the matter. He decides at last to say nothing till Baghdad is reached. But after that he will hold his tongue no longer."

"You think one of *us* is Long," said O'Rourke, still dazed. He drew a deep breath.

"It must be the Italian fellow—it *must*. . . . Or what about the Armenian?"

"To make up as a foreigner and get a foreign passport is really much more difficult than to remain English," said Mr. Parker Pyne.

"Miss Pryce?" cried O'Rourke incredulously.

"No," said Mr. Parker Pyne. "*This* is our man!"

He laid what seemed an almost friendly hand on the shoulder of the man beside him. But there was nothing friendly in his voice, and the fingers were vice-like in their grip.

"Squadron Leader Loftus or Mr. Samuel Long, it doesn't matter which you call him!"

"But that's impossible—impossible," spluttered O'Rourke. "Loftus has been in the service for years."

"But you've never met him before, have you? He was a stranger to all of you. It isn't the *real* Loftus naturally."

The quiet man found his voice.

"Clever of you to guess. How did you, by the way?"

"Your ridiculous statement that Smethurst had been killed by bumping his head. O'Rourke put that idea into your head when we were standing talking in Damascus yesterday. You thought—how simple! You were the only doctor with us—whatever you said would be accepted. You'd got Loftus's kit. You'd got his instruments. It was easy to select a neat little tool for your purpose. You lean over to speak to him and as you are speaking you drive the little weapon home.

You talk a minute or two longer. It is dark in the car. Who will suspect?

"Then comes the discovery of the body. You give your verdict. But it does not go as easily as you thought. Doubts are raised. You fall back on a second line of defence. Williamson repeats the conversation he has overheard Smethurst having with you. It is taken to refer to Hensley and you add a damaging little invention of your own about a leakage in Hensley's department. And then I make a final test. I mention the sand and the socks. You are holding a handful of sand. I send you to find the socks so *that we may know the truth*. But by that I did not mean what you thought I meant. *I had already examined Hensley's socks*. There was no sand in either of them. You put it there."

Mr. Samuel Long lit a cigarette.

"I give it up," he said. "My luck's turned. Well, I had a good run while it lasted. They were getting hot on my trail when I reached Egypt. I came across Loftus. He was just going to join up in Baghdad—and he knew none of them there. It was too good a chance to be missed. I bought him. It cost me twenty thousand pounds. What was that to me? Then, by cursed ill luck, I run into Smethurst—an ass if there ever was one! He was my fag at Eton. He had a bit of hero worship for me in those days. He didn't like the idea of giving me away. I did my best and at last he promised to say nothing till we reached Baghdad. What chance should I have then? None at all. There was only one way—to eliminate him. But I can assure you I am not a murderer by nature. My talents lie in quite another direction."

His face changed—contracted. He swayed and pitched forward.

O'Rourke bent over him.

"Probably prussic acid—in the cigarette," said Mr. Parker Pyne. "The gambler has lost his last throw."

He looked round him—at the wide desert. The sun beat down on him. Only yesterday they had left Damascus—by the Gate of Baghdad.

"Pass not beneath, O Caravan, or pass not singing. Have you heard
That silence where the birds are dead yet something pipeth like a bird?"

THE HOUSE AT SHIRAZ

It was six in the morning when Mr. Parker Pyne left for Persia after a stop in Baghdad.

The passenger space in the little monoplane was limited, and the small width of the seats was not such as to accommodate the bulk of Mr. Parker Pyne with anything like comfort. There were two fellow travellers—a large, florid man whom Mr. Parker Pyne judged to be of a talkative habit, and a thin woman with pursed-up lips and a determined air.

"At any rate," thought Mr. Parker Pyne, "they don't look as though they would want to consult me professionally."

Nor did they. The little woman was an American missionary, full of hard work and happiness, and the florid man was employed by an oil company. They had given their fellow traveller a résumé of their lives before the plane started.

"I am merely a tourist, I am afraid," Mr. Parker Pyne had said deprecatingly. "I am going to Teheran and Ispahan and Shiraz."

And the sheer music of the names enchanted him so much as he said them that he repeated them. Teheran. Ispahan. Shiraz.

Mr. Parker Pyne looked out at the country below him. It was flat desert. He felt the mystery of these vast, unpopulated regions.

At Kermanshah the machine came down for passport examinations and customs. A bag of Mr. Parker Pyne's was opened. A certain small cardboard box was scrutinised with some excitement. Questions were asked. Since Mr. Parker Pyne did not speak or understand Persian, the matter was difficult.

The pilot of the machine strolled up. He was a fair-haired young German, a fine-looking man, with deep-blue eyes and a weatherbeaten face. "Please?" he inquired pleasantly.

Mr. Parker Pyne, who had been indulging in some excellent realistic pantomime without, it seemed, much success, turned to him with relief. "It's bug powder," he said. "Do you think you could explain to them?"

The pilot looked puzzled. "Please?"

Mr. Parker Pyne repeated his plea in German. The pilot grinned and translated the sentence into Persian. The grave and sad officials were pleased; their sorrowful faces relaxed; they smiled. One even laughed. They found the idea humorous.

The three passengers took their places in the machine again and the flight continued. They swooped down at Hamadan to drop the mails, but the plane did not stop. Mr. Parker Pyne peered down, trying to see if he could distinguish the rock of Behistun, that romantic spot where Darius describes the extent of his empire and conquests in three different languages—Babylonian, Median and Persian.

It was one o'clock when they arrived at Teheran. There were more police formalities. The German pilot had come up and was standing by smiling as Mr. Parker Pyne finished answering a long interrogation which he had not understood.

"What have I said?" he asked of the German.

"That your father's Christian name is Tourist, that your profession is Charles, that the maiden name of your mother is Baghdad, and that you have come from Harriet."

"Does it matter?"

"Not the least in the world. Just answer something; that is all they need."

Mr. Parker Pyne was disappointed in Teheran. He found it distressingly modern. He said as much the following evening when he happened to run into Herr Schlagal, the pilot, just as he was entering his hotel. On an impulse he asked the other man to dine, and the German accepted.

The Georgian waiter hovered over them and issued his orders. The food arrived.

When they had reached the stage of *la tourte*, a somewhat sticky confection of chocolate, the German said:

"So you go to Shiraz?"

"Yes, I shall fly there. Then I shall come back from Shiraz to Ispahan and Teheran by road. Is it you who will fly me to Shiraz to-morrow?"

"*Ach*, no. I return to Baghdad."

"You have been long here?"

"Three years. It has only been established three years, our service. So far, we have never had an accident—*unberufen*!" He touched the table.

Thick cups of sweet coffee were brought. The two men smoked.

"My first passengers were two ladies," said the German reminiscently. "Two English ladies."

"Yes?" said Mr. Parker Pyne.

"The one she was a young lady very well born, the daughter of one of your ministers, the—how does one say it?—the Lady Esther Carr. She was handsome, very handsome, but mad."

"Mad?"

"Completely mad. She lives there at Shiraz in a big native house. She wears Eastern dress. She will see no Europeans. Is that a life for a well-born lady to live?"

"There have been others," said Mr. Parker Pyne. "There was Lady Hester Stanhope——"

"This one is mad," said the other abruptly. "You could see it in her eyes. Just so have I seen the eyes of my submarine commander in the war. He is now in an asylum."

Mr. Parker Pyne was thoughtful. He remembered Lord Micheldever, Lady Esther Carr's father, well. He had worked under him when the latter was Home Secretary—a big blond man with laughing blue eyes. He had seen Lady Micheldever once—a noted Irish beauty with her black hair and violet-blue eyes. They were both handsome, normal people, but for all that there *was* insanity in the Carr family. It cropped out every now and then, after missing a generation. It was odd, he thought, that Herr Schlagal should stress the point.

"And the other lady?" he asked idly.

"The other lady—is dead."

Something in his voice made Mr. Parker Pyne look up sharply.

"I have a heart," said Herr Schlagal. "I feel. She was, to me, most beautiful, that lady. You know how it is, these things come over you all of a sudden. She was a flower—a flower." He sighed deeply. "I went to see them once—at the house at Shiraz. The Lady Esther, she asked me to come. My little one, my flower, she was afraid of something, I could see it. When next I came back from Baghdad, I hear that she is dead. Dead!"

He paused and then said thoughtfully: "It might be that the other one killed her. She was mad, I tell you."

He sighed, and Mr. Parker Pyne ordered two Benedictines.

"The curaçao, it is good," said the Georgian waiter, and brought them two curaçaos.

Just after noon the following day, Mr. Parker Pyne had his first view of Shiraz. They had flown over mountain ranges with narrow, desolate valleys between, and all arid, parched, dry wilderness. Then suddenly Shiraz came into view—an emerald-green jewel in the heart of the wilderness.

Mr. Parker Pyne enjoyed Shiraz as he had not enjoyed Teheran. The primitive character of the hotel did not appal him, nor the equally primitive character of the streets.

He found himself in the midst of a Persian holiday. The Nan Ruz festival had begun on the previous evening—the fifteen-day period in which the Persians celebrate their New Years. He wandered through the empty bazaars and passed out into the great open stretch of common on the north side of the city. All Shiraz was celebrating.

One day he walked just outside the town. He had been to the tomb of Hafiz the poet, and it was on returning that he saw and was fascinated by a house. A house all tiled in blue and rose and yellow, set in a green garden with water and orange trees and roses. It was, he felt, the house of a dream.

That night he was dining with the English consul and he asked about the house.

"Fascinating place, isn't it? It was built by a former wealthy governor of Luristan, who had made a good thing out of his official position. An Englishwoman's got it now. You must have heard of her. Lady Esther Carr. Mad as a hatter. Gone completely native. Won't have anything to do with anything or anyone British."

"Is she young?"

"Too young to play the fool in this way. She's about thirty."

"There was another Englishwoman with her, wasn't there? A woman who died?"

"Yes; that was about three years ago. Happened the day after I took up my post here, as a matter of fact. Barham, my predecessor, died suddenly, you know."

"How did she die?" asked Mr. Parker Pyne bluntly.

"Fell from that courtyard or balcony place on the first floor. She was Lady Esther's maid or companion, I forget which. Anyway, she was carrying the breakfast tray and stepped back over the edge. Very sad; nothing to be done; cracked her skull on the stone below."

"What was her name?"

"King, I think; or was it Wills? No, that's the missionary woman. Rather a nice-looking girl."

"Was Lady Esther upset?"

"Yes—no, I don't know. She was very queer; I couldn't make her out. She's a very—well, imperious creature. You can see she is somebody, if you know what I mean; she rather scared me with her commanding ways and her dark, flashing eyes."

He laughed half-apologetically, then looked curiously at his companion. Mr. Parker Pyne was apparently staring into space. The match he had just struck to light his cigarette was burning away unheeded in his hand. It burned down to his fingers and he dropped it with an ejaculation of pain. Then he saw the consul's astonished expression and smiled.

"I beg your pardon," he said.

"Wool gathering, weren't you?"

"Three bags full," said Mr. Parker Pyne enigmatically.

They talked of other matters.

That evening, by the light of a small oil lamp, Mr. Parker Pyne wrote a letter. He hesitated a good deal over its composition. Yet in the end it was very simple:

> Mr. Parker Pyne presents his compliments to Lady Esther Carr and begs to state that he is staying at the Hotel Fars for the next three days should she wish to consult him.

He enclosed a cutting—the famous advertisement:

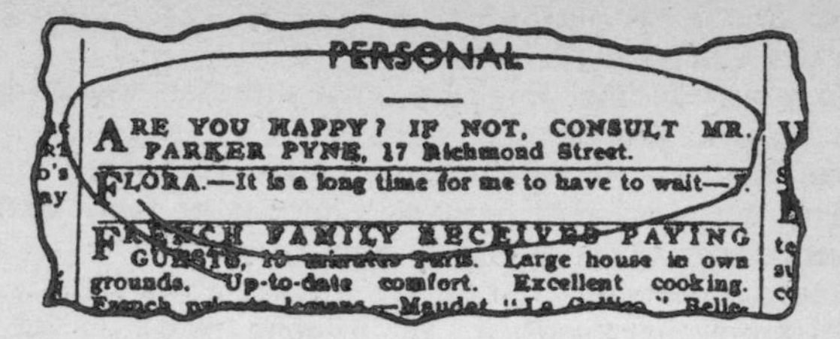

PERSONAL

ARE YOU HAPPY? IF NOT, CONSULT MR. PARKER PYNE, 17 Richmond Street.

FLORA.—It is a long time for me to have to wait—.

FRENCH FAMILY RECEIVES PAYING GUESTS, [illegible] Paris. Large house in own grounds. Up-to-date comfort. Excellent cooking. French [illegible]

"That ought to do the trick," said Mr. Parker Pyne, as he got gingerly into his rather uncomfortable bed. "Let me see, nearly three years; yes, it ought to do it."

On the following day about four o'clock the answer came. It was brought by a Persian servant who knew no English.

Lady Esther Carr will be glad if Mr. Parker Pyne will call upon her at nine o'clock this evening.

Mr. Parker Pyne smiled.

It was the same servant who received him that evening. He was taken through the dark garden and up an outside staircase that led round to the back of the house. From there a door was opened and he passed through into the central court or balcony, which was open to the night. A big divan was placed against the wall and on it reclined a striking figure.

Lady Esther was attired in Eastern robes, and it might have been suspected that one reason for her preference lay in the fact that they suited her rich, Oriental style of beauty. Imperious, the consul had called her, and indeed imperious she looked. Her chin was held high and her brows were arrogant.

"You are Mr. Parker Pyne? Sit down there."

Her hand pointed to a heap of cushions. On the third finger there flashed a big emerald carved with the arms of her family. It was an heirloom and must be worth a small fortune, Mr. Parker Pyne reflected.

He lowered himself obediently, though with a little difficulty. For a man of his figure it is not easy to sit on the ground gracefully.

A servant appeared with coffee. Mr. Parker Pyne took his cup and sipped appreciatively.

His hostess had acquired the Oriental habit of infinite

leisure. She did not rush into conversation. She, too, sipped her coffee with half-closed eyes. At last she spoke.

"So you help unhappy people," she said. "At least, that is what your advertisement claims."

"Yes."

"Why did you send it to me? Is it your way of—doing business on your travels?"

There was something decidedly offensive in her voice, but Mr. Parker Pyne ignored it. He answered simply, "No. My idea in travelling is to have a complete holiday from business."

"Then why send it to me?"

"Because I had reason to believe that you—are unhappy."

There was a moment's silence. He was very curious. How would she take that? She gave herself a minute to decide that point. Then she laughed.

"I suppose you thought that anyone who leaves the world, who lives as I do, cut off from my race, from my country, must do so because she is unhappy! Sorrow, disappointment—you think something like that drove me into exile? Oh, well, how should you understand? There—in England—I was a fish out of water. Here I am myself. I am an Oriental at heart. I love this seclusion. I dare say you can't understand that. To you, I must seem "—she hesitated a moment—"mad."

"You're not mad," said Mr. Parker Pyne.

There was a good deal of quiet assurance in his voice. She looked at him curiously.

"But they've been saying I am, I suppose. Fools! It takes all kinds to make a world. I'm perfectly happy."

"And yet you told me to come here," said Mr. Parker Pyne.

"I will admit I was curious to see you." She hesitated. "Besides, I never want to go back there—to England—but all the same, sometimes I like to hear what is going on in——"

"In the world you have left?"

She acknowledged the sentence with a nod.

Mr. Parker Pyne began to talk. His voice, mellow and reassuring, began quietly, then rose ever so little as he emphasised this point and that.

He talked of London, of society gossip, of famous men and women, of new restaurants and new night clubs, of race meetings and shooting parties and country-house scandals. He talked of clothes, of fashions from Paris, of little shops in unfashionable streets where marvellous bargains could be had.

He described theatres and cinemas, he gave film news, he described the building of new garden suburbs, he talked of bulbs and gardening, and he came last to a homely description of London in the evening, with the trams and the buses and the hurrying crowds going homeward after the day's work and of the little homes awaiting them, and of the whole strange intimate pattern of English family life.

It was a very remarkable performance, displaying as it did wide and unusual knowledge and a clever marshalling of the facts. Lady Esther's head had drooped; the arrogance of her poise had been abandoned. For some time her tears had been quietly falling, and now that he had finished, she abandoned all pretence and wept openly.

Mr. Parker Pyne said nothing. He sat there watching her. His face had the quiet, satisfied expression of one who has conducted an experiment and obtained the desired result.

She raised her head at last. "Well," she said bitterly, "are you satisfied?"

"I think so—now."

"How shall I bear it; how shall I bear it? Never to leave here; never to see—anyone again!" The cry came as though wrung out of her. She caught herself up, flushing. "Well?" she demanded fiercely. "Aren't you going to make the obvious remark? Aren't you going to say, 'If you want to go home so much, why not do so?'"

"No." Mr. Parker Pyne shook his head. "It's not nearly so easy as that for you."

For the first time a little look of fear crept into her eyes. "Do you know why I can't go?"

"I think so."

"Wrong." She shook her head. "The reason I can't go is a reason you'd never guess."

"I don't guess," said Mr. Parker Pyne. "I observe—and I classify."

She shook her head. "You don't know anything at all."

"I shall have to convince you, I see," said Mr. Parker

Pyne pleasantly. "When you came out here, Lady Esther, you flew, I believe, by the new German Air Service from Baghdad."

"Yes?"

"You were flown by a young pilot, Herr Schlagal, who afterwards came here to see you."

"Yes."

A different "yes" in some indescribable way—a softer "yes."

"And you had a friend, or companion, who—died." A voice like steel now—cold, offensive.

"My companion."

"Her name was——?"

"Muriel King."

"Were you fond of her?"

"What do you mean, fond?" She paused, checked herself. "She was useful to me."

She said it haughtily and Mr. Parker Pyne was reminded of the consul's saying: "You can see she is somebody, if you know what I mean."

"Were you sorry when she died?"

"I—naturally! Really, Mr. Pyne, is it necessary to go into all this?" She spoke angrily, and went on without waiting for an answer: "It has been very good of you to come. But I am a little tired. If you will tell me what I owe you——?"

But Mr. Parker Pyne did not move. He showed no signs of taking offence. He went quietly on with his questions. "Since she died, Herr Schlagal has not been to see you. Suppose he were to come, would you receive him?"

"Certainly not."

"You refuse absolutely?"

"Absolutely. Herr Schlagal will not be admitted."

"Yes," said Mr. Parker Pyne thoughtfully. "You could not say anything else."

The defensive armour of her arrogance broke down a little. She said uncertainly: "I—I don't know what you mean."

"Did you know, Lady Esther, that young Schlagal fell in love with Muriel King? He is a sentimental young man. He still treasures her memory."

"Does he?" Her voice was almost a whisper.

"What was she like?"

"What do you mean, what was she like? How do I know?"

"You must have looked at her sometimes," said Mr. Parker Pyne mildly.

"Oh, that! She was quite a nice-looking young woman."

"About your own age?"

"Just about." There was a pause, and then she said:

"Why do you think that—that Schlagal cared for her?"

"Because he told me so. Yes, yes, in the most unmistakable terms. As I say, he is a sentimental young man. He was glad to confide in me. He was very upset at her dying the way she did."

Lady Esther sprang to her feet. "Do you believe I murdered her?"

Mr. Parker Pyne did not spring to his feet. He was not a springing kind of man.

"No, my dear child," he said. "I do *not* believe that you murdered her, and that being so, I think the sooner you stop this play-acting and go home, the better."

"What do you mean, play-acting?"

"The truth is, you lost your nerve. Yes, you did. You lost your nerve badly. You thought you'd be accused of murdering your employer."

The girl made a sudden movement.

Mr. Parker Pyne went on. "You are not Lady Esther Carr. I knew that before I came here, but I've tested you to make sure." His smile broke out, bland and benevolent. "When I said my little piece just now, I was watching you, and every time you reacted *as Muriel King,* not as Esther Carr. The cheap shops, the cinemas, the new garden suburbs, going home by bus and tram—you reacted to all those. Country-house gossip, new night clubs, the chatter of Mayfair, race meetings—none of those meant anything at all to you."

His voice became even more persuasive and fatherly. "Sit down and tell me about it. You didn't murder Lady Esther, but you thought you might be accused of doing so. Just tell me how it all came about."

She took a long breath; then she sank down once more on the divan and began to speak. Her words came hurriedly, in little bursts.

"I must begin—at the beginning. I—I was afraid of her. She was mad—not quite mad—just a little. She brought me out here with her. Like a fool I was delighted; I thought it was so romantic. Little fool. That's what I was, a little fool. There was some business about a chauffeur. She was man-mad—absolutely man-mad. He wouldn't have anything to do with her, and it got out; her friends got to know about it and laughed. And she broke loose from her family and came out here.

"It was all a pose to save her face—solitude in the desert—all that sort of thing. She would have kept it up for a bit, and then gone back. But she got queerer and queerer. And there was the pilot. She—she took a fancy to him. He came here to see me, and she thought—— Oh, well, you can understand. But he must have made it clear to her. . . .

"And then she suddenly turned on me. She was awful, frightening. She said I should never go home again. She said I was in her power. She said I was a slave. Just that—a slave. She had the power of life and death over me."

Mr. Parker Pyne nodded. He saw the situation unfolding. Lady Esther slowly going over the edge of sanity, as others of her family had gone before her, and the frightened girl, ignorant and untravelled, believing everything that was said to her.

"But one day something in me seemed to snap. I stood up to her. I told her that if it came to it I was stronger than she was. I told her I'd throw her down on to the stones below. She was frightened, really frightened. I suppose she'd just thought me a worm. I took a step toward her—I don't know what she thought I meant to do. She moved backwards; she—she stepped back off the edge!" Muriel King buried her face in her hands.

"And then?" Mr. Parker Pyne prompted gently.

"I lost my head. I thought they'd say I'd pushed her over. I thought nobody would listen to me. I thought I should be thrown into some awful prison out here." Her lips worked. Mr. Parker Pyne saw clearly enough the unreasoning fear that had possessed her. "And then it came to me—if it were I! I knew that there would be a new British consul who'd never seen either of us. The other one had died.

"I thought I could manage the servants. To them we were

two mad Englishwomen. When one was dead, the other carried on. I gave them good presents of money and told them to send for the British consul. He came and I received him as Lady Esther. I had her ring on my finger. He was very nice and arranged everything. Nobody seemed to have the least suspicion."

Mr. Parker Pyne nodded thoughtfully. The prestige of a famous name. Lady Esther Carr might be mad as a hatter, but she was still Lady Esther Carr.

"And then afterwards," continuel Muriel, "I wished I hadn't. I saw that I'd been quite mad myself. I was condemned to stay on here playing a part. I didn't see how I could ever get away. If I confessed the truth now, it would look more than ever as though I'd murdered her. Oh, Mr. Pyne, what shall I do? What shall I do?"

"Do?" Mr. Parker Pyne rose to his feet as briskly as his figure allowed. "My dear child, you will come with me now to the British consul, who is a very amiable and kindly man. There will be certain unpleasant formalities to go through. I don't promise you that it will be all plain sailing, but you won't be hanged for murder. By the way, why was the breakfast tray found with the body?"

"I threw it over. I—I thought it would look more like me to have a tray there. Was it silly of me?"

"It was rather a clever touch," said Mr. Parker Pyne. "In fact, it was the one point which made me wonder if you might, perhaps, have done away with Lady Esther—that is, until I saw you. When I saw you, I knew that whatever else you might do in your life, you would never kill anyone."

"Because I haven't the nerve, you mean?"

"Your reflexes wouldn't work that way," said Mr. Parker Pyne, smiling. "Now, shall we go? There's an unpleasant job to be faced, but I'll see you through it, and then—home to Streatham Hill—it is Streatham Hill, isn't it? Yes, I thought so. I saw your face contract when I mentioned one particular bus number. Are you coming, my dear?"

Muriel King hung back. "They'll never believe me," she said nervously. "Her family and all. They wouldn't believe she could act the way she did."

"Leave it to me," said Mr. Parker Pyne. "I know something of the family history, you see. Come, child, don't go on playing the coward. Remember, there's a young man in Teheran sighing his heart out. We had better arrange that it is in his plane you fly to Baghdad."

The girl smiled and blushed. "I'm ready," she said simply. Then as she moved towards the door, she turned back. "You said you knew I was not Lady Esther Carr before you saw me. How could you possibly tell that?"

"Statistics," said Mr. Parker Pyne.

"Statistics?"

"Yes. Both Lord and Lady Micheldever had blue eyes. When the consul mentioned that their daughter had flashing *dark* eyes I knew there was something wrong. Brown-eyed people may produce a blue-eyed child, but not the other way about. A scientific fact, I assure you."

"I think you're wonderful!" said Muriel King.

THE PEARL OF PRICE

The party had had a long and tiring day. They had started from Amman early in the morning with a temperature of ninety-eight in the shade, and had come at last just as it was growing dark into the camp situated in the heart of that city of fantastic and preposterous red rock which is Petra.

There were seven of them, Mr. Caleb P. Blundell, that stout and prosperous American magnate. His dark and good-looking, if somewhat taciturn, secretary, Jim Hurst. Sir Donald Marvel, M.P., a tired-looking English politician. Doctor Carver, a world-renowned elderly archæologist. A gallant Frenchman, Colonel Dubosc, on leave from Syria. A Mr. Parker Pyne, not perhaps so plainly labelled with his profession, but breathing an atmosphere of British solidity. And lastly, there was Miss Carol Blundell—pretty, spoiled, and extremely sure of herself as the only woman among half a dozen men.

They dined in the big tent, having selected their tents or caves for sleeping in. They talked of politics in the Near East—the Englishman cautiously, the Frenchman discreetly, the American somewhat fatuously, and the archæologist and Mr. Parker Pyne not at all. Both of them, it seemed, preferred the rôle of listeners. So also did Jim Hurst.

Then they talked of the city they had come to visit.

"It's just too romantic for words," said Carol. "To think of those—what do you call 'em?—Nabatæans living here all that while ago, almost before time began!"

"Hardly that," said Mr. Parker Pyne mildly. "Eh, Doctor Carver?"

"Oh, that's an affair of a mere two thousand years back, and if racketeers are romantic, then I suppose the Nabatæans are too. They were a pack of wealthy blackguards, I should say, who compelled travellers to use their own caravan routes, and saw to it that all other routes were unsafe. Petra was the storehouse of their racketeering profits."

"You think they were just robbers?" asked Carol. "Just common thieves?"

"Thieves is a less romantic word, Miss Blundell. A thief suggests a petty pilferer. A robber suggests a larger canvas."

"What about a modern financier?" suggested Mr. Parker Pyne with a twinkle.

"That's one for you, Pop!" said Carol.

"A man who makes money benefits mankind," said Mr. Blundell sententiously.

"Mankind," murmured Mr. Parker Pyne, "is so ungrateful."

"What is honesty?" demanded the Frenchman. "It is a *nuance,* a convention. In different countries it means different things. An Arab is not ashamed of stealing. He is not ashamed of lying. With him it is from *whom* he steals or to *whom* he lies that matters."

"That is the point of view—yes," agreed Carver.

"Which shows the superiority of the West over the East," said Blundell. "When these poor creatures get education ——"

Sir Donald entered languidly into the conversation. "Education is rather rot, you know. Teaches fellows a lot of useless things. And what I mean is, nothing alters what you are."

"You mean?"

"Well, what I mean to say is, for instance, once a thief always a thief."

There was a dead silence for a moment. Then Carol began talking feverishly about mosquitoes, and her father backed her up.

Sir Donald, a little puzzled, murmured to his neighbour, Mr. Parker Pyne: "Seems I dropped a brick—what?"

"Curious," said Mr. Parker Pyne.

Whatever momentary embarrassment had been caused, one person had quite failed to notice it. The archæologist had sat silent, his eyes dreamy and abstracted. When a pause came, he spoke suddenly and abruptly.

"You know," he said, "I agree with that—at anyrate, from the opposite point of view. A man's fundamentally honest, or he isn't. You can't get away from it."

"You don't believe that sudden temptation, for instance, will turn an honest man into a criminal?" asked Mr. Parker Pyne.

"Impossible!" said Carver.

Mr. Parker Pyne shook his head gently. "I wouldn't say impossible. You see, there are so many factors to take into account. There's the breaking point, for instance."

"What do you call the breaking point?" asked young Hurst, speaking for the first time. He had a deep, rather attractive voice.

"The brain is adjusted to carry so much weight. The thing that precipitates the crisis—that turns an honest man into a dishonest one—may be a mere trifle. That is why most crimes are absurd. The cause, nine times out of ten, is that trifle of overweight—the straw that breaks the camel's back."

"It is the psychology you talk there, my friend," said the Frenchman.

"If a criminal were a psychologist, what a criminal he could be!" said Mr. Parker Pyne. His voice dwelt lovingly on the idea. "When you think that of ten people you meet, at least nine of them can be induced to act in any way you please by applying the right stimulus."

"Oh, explain that!" cried Carol.

"There's the bullyable man. Shout loud enough at him—and he obeys. There's the contradictory man. Bully him the opposite way from that in which you want him to go. Then there's the suggestible person, the commonest type of all. Those are the people who have *seen* a motor, because they have heard a motor horn; who *see* a postman because they hear the rattle of the letter-box; who *see* a knife in a wound because they are *told* a man has been stabbed; or who will have *heard* the pistol if they are told a man has been shot."

"I guess no one could put that sort of stuff over on me," said Carol incredulously.

"You're too smart for that, honey," said her father.

"It is very true what you say," said the Frenchman reflectively. "The preconceived idea, it deceives the senses."

Carol yawned. "I'm going to my cave. I'm tired to death. Abbas Effendi said we had to start early to-morrow. He's going to take us up to the place of sacrifice—whatever that is."

"It's where they sacrifice young and beautiful girls," said Sir Donald.

"Mercy, I hope not! Well, good-night, all. Oh, I've dropped my ear-ring."

Colonel Dubosc picked it up from where it had rolled across the table and returned it to her.

"Are they real?" asked Sir Donald abruptly. Discourteous for the moment, he was staring at the two large solitaire pearls at her ears.

"They're real, all right," said Carol.

"Cost me eighty thousand dollars," said her father with relish. "And she screws them in so loosely that they fall off and roll about the table. Want to ruin me, girl?"

"I'd say it wouldn't ruin you even if you had to buy me a new pair," said Carol fondly.

"I guess it wouldn't," her father acquiesced. "I could buy you three pairs of ear-rings without noticing it in my bank balance." He looked proudly around.

"How nice for you!" said Sir Donald.

"Well, gentlemen, I think I'll turn in now," said Blundell. "Good-night." Young Hurst went with him.

The other four smiled at one another, as though in sympathy over some thought.

"Well," drawled Sir Donald, "it's nice to know he

wouldn't miss the money. Purse-proud hog!" he added viciously.

"They have too much money, these Americans," said Dubosc.

"It is difficult," said Mr. Parker Pyne gently, "for a rich man to be appreciated by the poor."

Dubosc laughed. "Envy and malice?" he suggested. "You are right, Monsieur. We all wish to be rich; to buy the pearl ear-rings several times over. Except, perhaps, Monsieur here."

He bowed to Doctor Carver who, as seemed usual with him, was once more far away. He was fiddling with a little object in his hand.

"Eh?" He roused himself. "No, I must admit I don't covet large pearls. Money is always useful, of course." His tone put it where it belonged. "But look at this," he said. "Here is something a hundred times more interesting than pearls."

"What is it?"

"It's a cylinder seal of black hematite and it's got a presentation scene engraved on it—a god introducing a suppliant to a more enthroned god. The suppliant is carrying a kid by way of an offering, and the august god on the throne has the flies kept off him by a flunkey who wields a palm-branch fly whisk. That neat inscription mentions the man as a servant of Hammurabi, so that it must have been made just four thousand years ago."

He took a lump of plasticine from his pocket and smeared some on the table, then he oiled it with a little vaseline and pressed the seal upon it, rolling it out. Then, with a penknife, he detached a square of the plasticine and levered it gently up from the table.

"You see?" he said.

The scene he had described was unrolled before them in the plasticine, clear and sharply defined.

For a moment the spell of the past was laid upon them all. Then, from outside, the voice of Mr. Blundell was raised unmusically.

"Say, you niggers! Change my baggage out of this darned cave and into a tent! The no-see-ums are biting good and hard. I shan't get a wink of sleep."

"No-see-ums?" Sir Donald queried.

"Probably sand flies," said Doctor Carver.

"I like no-see-ums," said Mr. Parker Pyne. "It's a much more suggestive name."

The party started early the following morning, getting under way after various exclamations at the colour and marking of the rocks. The "rose-red" city was indeed a freak invented by Nature in her most extravagant and colourful mood. The party proceeded slowly, since Doctor Carver walked with his eyes bent on the ground, occasionally pausing to pick up small objects.

"You can always tell the archæologist—so," said Colonel Dubosc, smiling. "He regards never the sky, nor the hills, nor the beauties of nature. He walks with head bent, searching."

"Yes, but what for?" said Carol. "What are the things you are picking up, Doctor Carver?"

With a slight smile the archæologist held out a couple of muddy fragments of pottery.

"That rubbish!" cried Carol scornfully.

"Pottery is more interesting than gold," said Doctor Carver. Carol looked disbelieving.

They came to a sharp bend and passed two or three rock-cut tombs. The ascent was somewhat trying. The Bedouin guards went ahead, swinging up the precipitous slopes unconcernedly, without a downward glance at the sheer drop on one side of them.

Carol looked rather pale. One guard leaned down from above and extended a hand. Hurst sprang up in front of her and held out his stick like a rail on the precipitous side. She thanked him with a glance, and a minute later stood safely on a broad path of rock. The others followed slowly. The sun was now high and the heat was beginning to be felt.

At last they reached a broad plateau almost at the top. An easy climb led to the summit of a big square block of rock. Blundell signified to the guide that the party would go up alone. The Bedouins disposed themselves comfortably against the rocks and began to smoke. A few short minutes and the others had reached the summit.

It was a curious, bare place. The view was marvellous,

embracing the valley on every side. They stood on a plain rectangular floor, with rock basins cut in the side and a kind of sacrificial altar.

"A heavenly place for sacrifices," said Carol with enthusiasm. "But my, they must have had a time getting the victims up here!"

"There was originally a kind of zigzag rock road," explained Doctor Carver. "We shall see traces of it as we go down the other way."

They were some time longer commenting and talking. Then there was a tiny chink, and Doctor Carver said:

"I believe you've dropped your ear-ring again, Miss Blundell."

Carol clapped a hand to her ear. "Why, so I have."

Dubosc and Hurst began searching about.

"It must be just here," said the Frenchman. "It can't have rolled away, because there is nowhere for it to roll to. The place is like a square box."

"It can't have rolled into a crack?" queried Carol.

"There's not a crack anywhere," said Mr. Parker Pyne. "You can see for yourself. The place is perfectly smooth. Ah, you have found something, colonel?"

"Only a little pebble," said Dubosc, smiling and throwing it away."

Gradually a different spirit—a spirit of tension—came over the search. They were not said aloud, but the words "eighty thousand dollars" were present in everybody's mind.

"You are sure you had it, Carol?" snapped her father. "I mean, perhaps you dropped it on the way up."

"I had it just as we stepped on to the plateau here," said Carol. "I know, because Doctor Carver pointed out to me that it was loose and he screwed it up for me. That's so, isn't it, doctor?"

Doctor Carver assented. It was Sir Donald who voiced the thoughts in everybody's mind.

"This is rather an unpleasant business, Mr. Blundell," he said. "You were telling us last night what the value of these ear-rings is. One of them alone is worth a small fortune. If this ear-ring is not found, and it does not look as though it will be found, every one of us will be under a certain suspicion."

"And for one, I ask to be searched," broke in Colonel Dubosc. "I do not ask, I demand it as a right!"

"You search me too," said Hurst. His voice sounded harsh.

"What does everyone else feel?" asked Sir Donald, looking around.

"Certainly," said Mr. Parker Pyne.

"An excellent idea," said Doctor Carver.

"I'll be in on this too, gentlemen," said Mr. Blundell. "I've got my reasons, though I don't want to stress them."

"Just as you like, of course, Mr. Blundell," said Sir Donald courteously.

"Carol, my dear, will you go down and wait with the guides?"

Without a word the girl left them. Her face was set and grim. There was a despairing look upon it that caught the attention of one member of the party, at least. He wondered just what it meant.

The search proceeded. It was drastic and thorough—and completely unsatisfactory. One thing was certain. No one was carrying the ear-ring on his person. It was a subdued little troop that negotiated the descent and listened half-heartedly to the guide's descriptions and information.

Mr. Parker Pyne had just finished dressing for lunch when a figure appeared at the door of his tent.

"Mr. Pyne, may I come in?"

"Certainly, my dear young lady, certainly."

Carol came in and sat down on the bed. Her face had the same grim look upon it that he had noticed earlier in the day.

"You pretend to straighten out things for people when they are unhappy, don't you?" she demanded.

"I am on holiday, Miss Blundell. I am not taking any cases."

"Well, you're going to take this one," said the girl calmly. "Look here, Mr. Pyne, I'm just as wretched as anyone could well be."

"What is troubling you?" he asked. "Is it this business of the ear-ring?"

"That's just it. You've said it. Jim Hurst didn't take it, Mr. Pyne. I know he didn't."

"I don't quite follow you, Miss Blundell. Why should anyone assume he had?"

"Because of his record. Jim Hurst was once a thief, Mr. Pyne. He was caught in our house. I—I was sorry for him. He looked so young and desperate——"

"And so good-looking," thought Mr. Parker Pyne.

"I persuaded Pop to give him a chance to make good. My father will do anything for me. Well, he gave Jim his chance and Jim has made good. Father's come to rely on him and to trust him with all his business secrets. And in the end he'll come around altogether, or would have if this hadn't happened."

"When you say 'come around'——?"

"I mean that I want to marry Jim and he wants to marry me."

"And Sir Donald?"

"Sir Donald is Father's idea. He's not mine. Do you think I want to marry a stuffed fish like Sir Donald?"

Without expressing any views as to this description of the young Englishman, Mr. Parker Pyne asked: "And Sir Donald himself?"

"I dare say he thinks I'd be good for his impoverished acres," said Carol scornfully.

Mr. Parker Pyne considered the situation. "I should like to ask you about two things," he said. "Last night the remark was made, 'once a thief, always a thief.'"

The girl nodded.

"I see now the reason for the embarrassment that remark seemed to cause."

"Yes, it was awkward for Jim—and for me and Pop too. I was so afraid Jim's face would show something that I just trotted out the first remarks I could think of."

Mr. Parker Pyne nodded thoughtfully. Then he asked: "Just why did your father insist on being searched to-day?"

"You didn't get that? I did. Pop had it in his mind that I might think the whole business was a frame-up against Jim. You see, he's crazy for me to marry the Englishman. Well, he wanted to show me that he hadn't done the dirty on Jim."

"Dear me," said Mr. Parker Pyne, "this is all very illuminating. In a general sense, I mean. It hardly helps us in our particular inquiry."

"You're not going to hand in your checks?"

"No, no." He was silent a moment, then he said: "What is it exactly you want me to do, Miss Carol?"

"Prove it wasn't Jim who took that pearl."

"And suppose—excuse me—that it was?"

"If you think so, you're wrong—dead wrong."

"Yes, but have you really considered the case carefully? Don't you think that the pearl might prove a sudden temptation to Mr. Hurst? The sale of it would bring in a large sum of money—a foundation on which to speculate, shall we say?—which will make him independent, so that he can marry you with or without your father's consent."

"Jim didn't do it," said the girl simply.

This time Mr. Parker Pyne accepted her statement. "Well, I'll do my best."

She nodded abruptly and left the tent. Mr. Parker Pyne in his turn sat down on the bed. He gave himself up to thought. Suddenly he chuckled.

"I'm growing slow-witted," he said aloud. At lunch he was very cheerful.

The afternoon passed peacefully. Most people slept. When Mr. Parker Pyne came into the big tent at a quarter-past four only Doctor Carver was there. He was examining some fragments of pottery.

"Ah!" said Mr. Parker Pyne, drawing up a chair to the table. "Just the man I want to see. Can you let me have that bit of plasticine you carry about?"

The doctor felt in his pockets and produced a stick of plasticine, which he offered to Mr. Parker Pyne.

"No," said Mr. Parker Pyne, waving it away, "that's not the one I want. I want that lump you had last night. To be frank, it's not the plasticine I want. It's the contents of it."

There was a pause, and then Doctor Carver said quietly, "I don't think I quite understand you."

"I think you do," said Mr. Parker Pyne. "I want Miss Blundell's pearl ear-ring."

There was a minute's dead silence. Then Carver slipped his hand into his pocket and took out a shapeless lump of plasticine.

"Clever of you," he said. His face was expressionless.

"I wish you'd tell me about it," said Mr. Parker Pyne.

His fingers were busy. With a grunt, he extracted a somewhat smeared pearl ear-ring. "Just curiosity, I know," he added apologetically. "But I should like to hear about it."

"I'll tell you," said Carver, "if you'd tell me just how you happened to pitch upon me. You didn't see anything, did you?"

Mr. Parker Pyne shook his head. "I just thought about it," he said.

"It was really sheer accident, to start with," said Carver. "I was behind you all this morning and I came across it lying in front of me—it must have fallen from the girl's ear a moment before. She hadn't noticed it. Nobody had. I picked it up and put it into my pocket, meaning to return it to her as soon as I caught her up. But I forgot.

"And then, half-way up that climb, I began to think. The jewel meant nothing to that fool of a girl—her father would buy her another without noticing the cost. And it would mean a lot to me. The sale of that pearl would equip an expedition." His impassive face suddenly twitched and came to life. "Do you know the difficulty there is nowadays in raising subscriptions for digging? No, you don't. The sale of that pearl would make everything easy. There's a site I want to dig—up in Baluchistan. There's a whole chapter of the past there waiting to be discovered. . . .

"What you said last night came into my mind—about a suggestible witness. I thought the girl was that type. As we reached the summit I told her her ear-ring was loose. I pretended to tighten it. What I really did was to press the point of a small pencil into her ear. A few minutes later I dropped a little pebble. She was quite ready to swear then that the ear-ring had been in her ear and had just dropped off. In the meantime I pressed the pearl into a lump of plasticine in my pocket. That's my story. Not a very edifying one. Now for your turn."

"There isn't much of my story," said Mr. Parker Pyne. "You were the only man who'd picked up things from the ground—that's what made me think of you. And finding that little pebble was significant. It suggested the trick you'd played. And then——"

"Go on," said Carver.

"Well, you see, you'd talked about honesty a little too

vehemently last night. Protesting overmuch—well, you know what Shakespeare says. It looked, somehow, as though you were trying to convince *yourself*. And you were a little too scornful about money."

The face of the man in front of him looked lined and weary. "Well, that's that," he said. "It's all up with me now. You'll give the girl back her geegaw, I suppose? Odd thing, the barbaric instinct for ornamentation. You find it going back as far as paleolithic times. One of the first instincts of the female sex."

"I think you misjudge Miss Carol," said Mr. Parker Pyne. "She has brains—and what is more, a heart. I think she will keep this business to herself."

"Father won't, though," said the archæologist.

"I think he will. You see, 'Pop' has his own reasons for keeping quiet. There's no forty-thousand-dollar touch about this ear-ring. A mere fiver would cover its value."

"You mean——?"

"Yes. The girl doesn't know. She thinks they are genuine, all right. I had my suspicions last night. Mr. Blundell talked a little too much about all the money he had. When things go wrong and you're caught in the slump—well, the best thing to do is to put a good face on it and bluff. Mr. Blundell was bluffing."

Suddenly Doctor Carver grinned. It was an engaging small-boy grin, strange to see on the face of an elderly man. "Then we're all poor devils together," he said.

"Exactly," said Mr. Parker Pyne and quoted, "'A fellow feeling makes us wondrous kind.'"

DEATH ON THE NILE

Lady Grayle was nervous. From the moment of coming on board the S.S. *Fayoum* she complained of everything. She did not like her cabin. She could bear the morning sun, but not the afternoon sun. Pamela Grayle, her niece, obligingly gave up her cabin on the other side. Lady Grayle accepted it grudgingly.

She snapped at Miss MacNaughton, her nurse, for having

given her the wrong scarf and for having packed her little pillow instead of leaving it out. She snapped at her husband, Sir George, for having just bought her the wrong strings of beads. It was lapis she wanted, not carnelian. George was a fool!

Sir George said anxiously, " Sorry, me dear, sorry. I'll go back and change 'em. Plenty of time."

She did not snap at Basil West, her husband's private secretary, because nobody ever snapped at Basil. His smile disarmed you before you began.

But the worst of it fell assuredly to the dragoman—an imposing and richly dressed personage whom nothing could disturb.

When Lady Grayle caught sight of a stranger in a basket chair and realised that he was a fellow passenger, the vials of her wrath were poured out like water.

" They told me distinctly at the office that we were the only passengers! It was the end of the season and there was no one else going!"

" That right, lady," said Mohammed calmly. " Just you and party and one gentleman, that's all."

" But I was told that there would be only ourselves."

" That quite right, lady."

" It's not all right! It was a lie! What is that man doing here?"

" He come later, lady. After you take tickets. He only decide come this morning."

" It's an absolute swindle!"

" That's all right, lady; him very quiet gentleman, very nice, very quiet."

" You're a fool! You know nothing about it. Miss MacNaughton, where are you? Oh, there you are. I've repeatedly asked you to stay near me. I might feel faint. Help me to my cabin and give me an aspirin, and don't let Mohammed come near me. He keeps on saying 'That right, lady,' till I feel I could scream."

Miss MacNaughton proffered an arm without a word.

She was a tall woman of about thirty-five, handsome in a quiet, dark way. She settled Lady Grayle in the cabin, propped her up with cushions, administered an aspirin and listened to the thin flow of complaint.

Lady Grayle was forty-eight. She had suffered since she was sixteen from the complaint of having too much money. She had married that impoverished baronet, Sir George Grayle, ten years before.

She was a big woman, not bad-looking as regarded features, but her face was fretful and lined, and the lavish make-up she applied only accentuated the blemishes of time and temper. Her hair had been in turn platinum-blond and henna-red, and was looking tired in consequence. She was overdressed and wore too much jewellery.

"Tell Sir George," she finished, while the silent Miss MacNaughton waited with an expressionless face—"tell Sir George that he *must* get that man off the boat! I *must* have privacy. All I've gone through lately——" She shut her eyes.

"Yes, Lady Grayle," said Miss MacNaughton, and left the cabin.

The offending last-minute passenger was still sitting in the deck-chair. He had his back to Luxor and was staring out across the Nile to where the distant hills showed golden above a line of dark green.

Miss MacNaughton gave him a swift, appraising glance as she passed.

She found Sir George in the lounge. He was holding a string of beads in his hand and looking at it doubtfully.

"Tell me, Miss MacNaughton, do you think these will be all right?"

Miss MacNaughton gave a swift glance at the lapis.

"Very nice indeed," she said.

"You think Lady Grayle will be pleased—eh?"

"Oh, no, I shouldn't say that, Sir George. You see, nothing *would* please her. That's the real truth of it. By the way, she sent me with a message to you. She wants you to get rid of this extra passenger."

Sir George's jaw dropped. "How can I? What could I say to the fellow?"

"Of course you can't." Elsie MacNaughton's voice was brisk and kindly. "Just say there was nothing to be done." She added encouragingly, "It will be all right."

"You think it will, eh?" His face was ludicrously pathetic.

Elsie MacNaughton's voice was still kinder as she said:

"You really must not take these things to heart, Sir George. It's just health, you know. Don't take it seriously."

"You think she's really bad, nurse?"

A shade crossed the nurse's face. There was something odd in her voice as she answered: "Yes, I—I don't quite like her condition. But please don't worry, Sir George. You mustn't. You really mustn't." She gave him a friendly smile and went out.

Pamela came in, very languid and cool in her white. "Hallo, Nunks."

"Hallo, Pam, me dear."

"What have you got there? Oh, nice!"

"Well, I'm glad you think so. Do you think your aunt will think so, too?"

"She's incapable of liking anything. I can't think why you married the woman, Nunks."

Sir George was silent. A confused panorama of unsuccessful racing, pressing creditors and a handsome if domineering woman rose before his mental vision.

"Poor old dear," said Pamela. "I suppose you had to do it. But she does give us both rather hell, doesn't she?"

"Since she's been ill——" began Sir George.

Pamela interrupted him.

"She's not ill! Not really. She can always do anything she wants to. Why, while you were up at Assouan she was as merry as a—a cricket. I bet you Miss MacNaughton knows she's a fraud."

"I don't know what we'd do without Miss MacNaughton," said Sir George, with a sigh.

"She's an efficient creature," admitted Pamela. "I don't exactly dote on her as you do, though, Nunks. Oh, you do! Don't contradict. You think she's wonderful. So she is, in a way. But she's a dark horse. I never know what she's thinking. Still, she manages the old cat quite well."

"Look here, Pam, you mustn't speak of your aunt like that. Dash it all, she's very good to you."

"Yes, she pays all our bills, doesn't she? It's the hell of a life, though."

Sir George passed on to a less painful subject. "What are we to do about this fellow who's coming on the trip? Your aunt wants the boat to herself."

"Well, she can't have it," said Pamela coolly. "The man's quite presentable. His name's Parker Pyne. I should think he was a civil servant out of the Records Department—if there is such a thing. Funny thing is, I seem to have heard the name somewhere. Basil!" The secretary had just entered. "Where have I seen the name Parker Pyne?"

"Front page of *The Times*. Agony Column," replied the young man promptly. "'Are you happy? If not, consult Mr. Parker Pyne.'"

"Never! How frightfully amusing! Let's tell him all our troubles all the way to Cairo."

"I haven't any," said Basil West simply. "We're going to glide down the golden Nile, and see temples"—he looked quickly at Sir George, who had picked up a paper—"together."

The last word was only just breathed, but Pamela caught it. Her eyes met his.

"You're right, Basil," she said lightly. "It's good to be alive."

Sir George got up and went out. Pamela's face clouded over.

"What's the matter, my sweet?"

"My detested aunt-by-marriage——"

"Don't worry," said Basil quickly. "What does it matter what she gets in her head? Don't contradict her. You see," he laughed, "it's good camouflage."

The benevolent figure of Mr. Parker Pyne entered the lounge. Behind him came the picturesque figure of Mohammed, prepared to say his piece.

"Lady, gentlemans, we start now. In a few minutes we pass temples of Karnak right-hand side. I tell you story now about little boy who went to buy a roasted lamb for his father . . ."

Mr. Parker Pyne mopped his forehead. He had just returned from a visit to the Temple of Dendera. Riding on a donkey was, he felt, an exercise ill suited to his figure. He was proceeding to remove his collar when a note propped up on the dressing table caught his attention. He opened it. It ran as follows:

Dear Sir,—I should be obliged if you should not visit

the Temple of Abydos, but would remain on the boat, as I wish to consult you.

Yours truly,

Ariadne Grayle

A smile creased Mr. Parker Pyne's large, bland face. He reached for a sheet of paper and unscrewed his fountain pen.

Dear Lady Grayle (he wrote), I am sorry to disappoint you, but I am at present on holiday and am not doing any professional business.

He signed his name and dispatched the letter by a steward. As he completed his change of toilet, another note was brought to him.

Dear Mr. Parker Pyne,—I appreciate the fact that you are on holiday, but I am prepared to pay a fee of a hundred pounds for a consultation.

Yours truly,

Ariadne Grayle

Mr. Parker Pyne's eyebrows rose. He tapped his teeth thoughtfully with his fountain pen. He wanted to see Abydos, but a hundred pounds was a hundred pounds. And Egypt had been even more wickedly expensive than he had imagined.

Dear Lady Grayle (he wrote),—I shall not visit the Temple of Abydos.

Yours faithfully,

J. Parker Pyne

Mr. Parker Pyne's refusal to leave the boat was a source of great grief to Mohammed.

"Very nice temple. All my gentlemans like see that temple. I get you carriage. I get you chair and sailors carry you."

Mr. Parker Pyne refused all these tempting offers.

The others set off.

Mr. Parker Pyne waited on deck. Presently the door of Lady Grayle's cabin opened and the lady herself trailed out on deck.

"Such a hot afternoon," she observed graciously. "I see you have stayed behind, Mr. Pyne. Very wise of you. Shall we have some tea together in the lounge?"

Mr. Parker Pyne rose promptly and followed her. It cannot be denied that he was curious.

It seemed as though Lady Grayle felt some difficulty in

coming to the point. She fluttered from this subject to that. But finally she spoke in an altered voice.

"Mr. Pyne, what I am about to tell you is in the strictest confidence! You do understand that, don't you?"

"Naturally."

She paused, took a deep breath. Mr. Parker Pyne waited.

"I want to know whether or not my husband is poisoning me."

Whatever Mr. Parker Pyne had expected, it was not this. He showed his astonishment plainly. "That is a very serious accusation to make, Lady Grayle."

"Well, I'm not a fool and I wasn't born yesterday. I've had my suspicions for some time. Whenever George goes away I get better. My food doesn't disagree with me and I feel a different woman. There must be some reason for that."

"What you say is very serious, Lady Grayle. You must remember I am not a detective. I am, if you like to put it that way, a heart specialist——"

She interrupted him. "Eh—and don't you think it worries me, all this? It's not a policeman I want—I can look after myself, thank you—it's certainty I want. I've got to *know*. I'm not a wicked woman, Mr. Pyne. I act fairly by those who act fairly by me. A bargain's a bargain. I've kept my side of it. I've paid my husband's debts and I've not stinted him in money."

Mr. Parker Pyne had a fleeting pang of pity for Sir George.

"And as for the girl, she's had clothes and parties and this, that and the other. Common gratitude is all I ask."

"Gratitude is not a thing that can be produced to order, Lady Grayle."

"Nonsense!" said Lady Grayle. She went on: "Well, there it is! Find out the truth for me! Once I *know*——"

He looked at her curiously. "Once you know, what then, Lady Grayle?"

"That's my business." Her lips closed sharply

Mr. Parker Pyne hesitated a minute, then he said: "You will excuse me, Lady Grayle, but I have the impression that you are not being entirely frank with me."

"That's absurd. I've told you exactly what I want you to find out."

"Yes, but not the reason *why*?"

Their eyes met. Hers fell first.

"I should think the reason was self-evident," she said.

"No, because I am in doubt upon one point."

"What is that?"

"Do you want your suspicions proved right or wrong?"

"Really, Mr. Pyne!" The lady rose to her feet, quivering with indignation.

Mr. Parker Pyne nodded his head gently. "Yes, yes," he said. "But that doesn't answer my question, you know."

"Oh!" Words seemed to fail her. She swept out of the room.

Left alone, Mr. Parker Pyne became very thoughtful. He was so deep in his own thoughts that he started perceptibly when someone came in and sat down opposite him. It was Miss MacNaughton.

"Surely you're all back very soon," said Mr. Parker Pyne.

"The others aren't back. I said I had a headache and came back alone." She hesitated. "Where is Lady Grayle?"

"I should imagine lying down in her cabin."

"Oh, then that's all right. I don't want her to know I've come back."

"You didn't come back on her account, then?"

Miss MacNaughton shook her head. "No, I came back to see you."

Mr. Parker Pyne was surprised. He would have said offhand that Miss MacNaughton was eminently capable of looking after her troubles herself without seeking outside advice. It seemed that he was wrong.

"I've watched you since we all came on board. I think you're a person of wide experience and good judgment. And I want advice very badly."

"And yet—excuse me, Miss MacNaughton—but you're not the type that usually seeks advice. I should say that you were a person who was quite content to rely on her own judgment."

"Normally, yes. But I am in a very peculiar position." She hesitated a moment. "I do not usually talk about my cases. But in this instance I think it is necessary. Mr. Pyne, when I left England with Lady Grayle, she was a straightforward case. In plain language, there was nothing the matter with her. That's not quite true, perhaps. Too much leisure and too much money do produce a definite pathological condition. Having a few floors to scrub every day and five or six children to look after would have made Lady Grayle a perfectly healthy and a much happier woman."

Mr. Parker Pyne nodded.

"As a hospital nurse, one sees a lot of these nervous cases. Lady Grayle *enjoyed* her bad health. It was my part not to minimise her sufferings, to be as tactful as I could—and to enjoy the trip myself as much as possible."

"Very sensible," said Mr. Parker Pyne.

"But, Mr. Pyne, things are not as they were. The suffering that Lady Grayle complains of now is real and not imagined."

"You mean?"

"I have come to suspect that Lady Grayle is being poisoned."

"Since when have you suspected this?"

"For the past three weeks."

"Do you suspect—any particular person?"

Her eyes dropped. For the first time her voice lacked sincerity. "No."

"I put it to you, Miss MacNaughton, that you do suspect one particular person, and that that person is Sir George Grayle."

"Oh, no, no, I can't believe it of him! He is so pathetic, so child-like. He couldn't be a cold-blooded poisoner." Her voice had an anguished note in it.

"And yet you have noticed that whenever Sir George is absent his wife is better and that her periods of illness correspond with his return."

She did not answer.

"What poison do you suspect? Arsenic?"

"Something of that kind. Arsenic or antimony."

"And what steps have you taken?"

"I have done my utmost to supervise what Lady Grayle eats and drinks."

Mr. Parker Pyne nodded. "Do you think Lady Grayle has any suspicion herself?" he asked casually.

"Oh, no, I'm sure she hasn't."

"There you are wrong," said Mr. Parker Pyne. "Lady Grayle *does* suspect."

Miss MacNaughton showed her astonishment.

"Lady Grayle is more capable of keeping a secret than you imagine," said Mr. Parker Pyne. "She is a woman who knows how to keep her own counsel very well."

"That surprises me very much," said Miss MacNaughton slowly.

"I should like to ask you one more question, Miss MacNaughton. Do you think Lady Grayle likes you?"

"I've never thought about it."

They were interrupted. Mohammed came in, his face beaming, his robes flowing behind him.

"Lady, she hear you come back; she ask for you. She say why you not come to her?"

Elsie MacNaughton rose hurriedly. Mr. Parker Pyne rose also.

"Would a consultation early to-morrow morning suit you?" he asked.

"Yes, that would be the best time. Lady Grayle sleeps late. In the meantime, I shall be very careful."

"I think Lady Grayle will be careful too."

Miss MacNaughton disappeared.

Mr. Parker Pyne did not see Lady Grayle till just before dinner. She was sitting smoking a cigarette and burning what seemed to be a letter. She took no notice at all of him, by which he gathered that she was still offended.

After dinner he played bridge with Sir George, Pamela and Basil. Everyone seemed a little distrait, and the bridge game broke up early.

It was some hours later when Mr. Parker Pyne was roused. It was Mohammed who came to him.

"Old lady, she very ill. Nurse, she very frightened. I try to get doctor."

Mr. Parker Pyne hurried on some clothes. He arrived at the doorway of Lady Grayle's cabin at the same time as Basil West. Sir George and Pamela were inside. Elsie MacNaughton was working desperately over her patient. As Mr. Parker Pyne arrived, a final convulsion seized the poor lady. Her arched body writhed and stiffened. Then she fell back on her pillows.

Mr. Parker Pyne drew Pamela gently outside.

"How awful!" the girl was half-sobbing. "How awful! Is she, is she——?"

"Dead? Yes, I am afraid it is all over."

He put her into Basil's keeping. Sir George came out of the cabin, looking dazed.

"I never thought she was really ill," he was muttering. "Never thought it for a moment."

Mr. Parker Pyne pushed past him and entered the cabin.

Elsie MacNaughton's face was white and drawn. "They have sent for a doctor?" she asked.

"Yes." Then he said: "Strychnine?"

"Yes. Those convulsions are unmistakable. Oh, I can't believe it!" She sank into a chair, weeping. He patted her shoulder.

Then an idea seemed to strike him. He left the cabin hurriedly and went to the lounge. There was a little scrap of paper left unburnt in an ash-tray. Just a few words were distinguishable:

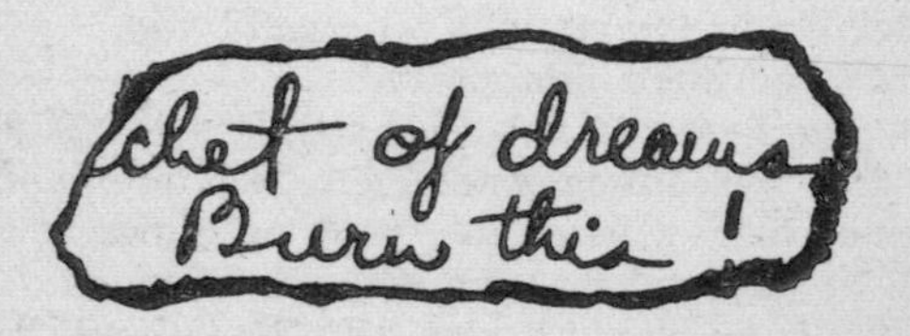

"Now, that's interesting," said Mr. Parker Pyne.

Mr. Parker Pyne sat in the room of a prominent Cairo official. "So that's the evidence," he said thoughtfully.

"Yes, pretty complete. Man must have been a damned fool."

"I shouldn't call Sir George a brainy man."

"All the same!" The other recapitulated: "Lady Grayle wants a cup of Bovril. The nurse makes it for her. Then she must have sherry in it. Sir George produces the sherry. Two hours later, Lady Grayle dies with unmistakable signs of strychnine poisoning. A packet of strychnine is found in Sir George's cabin and another packet actually in the pocket of his dinner jacket."

"Very thorough," said Mr. Parker Pyne. "Where did the strychnine come from, by the way?"

"There's a little doubt over that. The nurse had some—in case Lady Grayle's heart troubled her—but she's contradicted herself once or twice. First she said her supply was intact, and now she says it isn't."

"Very unlike her not to be sure," was Mr. Parker Pyne's comment.

"They were in it together, in my opinion. They've got a weakness for each other, those two."

"Possibly; but if Miss MacNaughton had been planning murder, she'd have done it a good deal better. She's an efficient young woman."

"Well, there it is. In my opinion, Sir George is in for it. He hasn't a dog's chance."

"Well, well," said Mr. Parker Pyne, "I must see what I can do."

He sought out the pretty niece.

Pamela was white and indignant. "Nunks never did such a thing—never—never—never!"

"Then who did?" said Mr. Parker Pyne placidly.

Pamela came nearer. "Do you know what I think? *She did it herself*. She's been frightfully queer lately. She used to imagine things."

"What things?"

"Queer things. Basil, for instance. She was always hinting that Basil was in love with her. And Basil and I are—we are——"

"I realise that," said Mr. Parker Pyne, smiling.

"All that about Basil was pure imagination. I think she had a down on poor little Nunks, and I think she made up that story and told it to you, and then put the strychnine in his cabin and in his pocket and poisoned herself. People have done things like that, haven't they?"

"They have," admitted Mr. Parker Pyne. "But I don't think that Lady Grayle did. She wasn't, if you'll allow me to say so, the type."

"But the delusions?"

"Yes, I'd like to ask Mr. West about that."

He found the young man in his room. Basil answered his questions readily enough.

"I don't want to sound fatuous, but she took a fancy to me. That's why I daren't let her know about me and Pamela. She'd have had Sir George fire me."

"You think Miss Grayle's theory a likely one?"

"Well, it's possible, I suppose." The young man was doubtful.

"But not good enough," said Mr. Parker Pyne quietly. "No, we must find something better." He became lost in meditation for a minute or two. "A confession would be best," he said briskly. He unscrewed his fountain pen and produced a sheet of paper. "Just write it out, will you?"

Basil West stared at him in amazement. "Me? What on earth do you mean?"

"My dear young man"—Mr. Parker Pyne sounded almost paternal—"I know all about it. How you made love to the good lady. How she had scruples. How you fell in love with the pretty, penniless niece. How you arranged your plot. Slow poisoning. It might pass for natural death from gastro-enteritis—if not, it would be laid to Sir George's doing, since you were careful to let the attacks coincide with his presence.

"Then your discovery that the lady was suspicious and had talked to me about the matter. Quick action! You abstracted some strychnine from Miss MacNaughton's store. Planted some of it in Sir George's cabin, and some in his pocket, and put sufficient into a cachet which you enclosed with a note to the lady, telling her it was a 'cachet of dreams.'

"A romantic idea. She'd take it as soon as the nurse had left her, and no one would know anything about it. But you made one mistake, my young man. It is useless asking a lady to burn letters. They never do. I've got all that pretty correspondence, including the one about the cachet."

Basil West had turned green. All his good looks had vanished. He looked like a trapped rat.

"Damn you!" he snarled. "So you know all about it. You damned interfering Nosey Parker."

Mr. Parker Pyne was saved from physical violence by the appearance of the witnesses he had thoughtfully arranged to have listening outside the half-closed door.

Mr. Parker Pyne was again discussing the case with his friend the high official.

"And I hadn't a shred of evidence! Only an almost indecipherable fragment, with '*Burn this!*' on it. I deduced the whole story and tried it on him. It worked. I'd stumbled on the truth. The letters did it. Lady Grayle had burned every scrap he wrote, but *he didn't know that*.

"She was really a very unusual woman. I was puzzled when she came to me. What she wanted was for me to tell her that her husband was poisoning her. In that case, she meant to go off with young West. But she wanted to act fairly. Curious character."

"That poor little girl is going to suffer," said the other.

"She'll get over it," said Mr. Parker Pyne callously. "She's young. I'm anxious that Sir George should get a little enjoyment before it's too late. He's been treated like a worm for ten years. Now, Elsie MacNaughton will be very kind to him."

He beamed. Then he sighed. "I am thinking of going incognito to Greece. I really *must* have a holiday!"

THE ORACLE AT DELPHI

Mrs. Willard J. Peters did not really care for Greece. And of Delphi she had, in her secret heart, no opinion at all.

Mrs. Peters' spiritual homes were Paris, London and the Riviera. She was a woman who enjoyed hotel life, but her idea of a hotel bedroom was a soft-pile carpet, a luxurious bed, a profusion of different arrangements of electric light, including a shaded bedside lamp, plenty of hot and cold water and a telephone beside the bed, by means of which you could order tea, meals, mineral waters, cocktails and speak to your friends.

In the hotel at Delphi there were none of these things. There was a marvellous view from the windows, the bed was clean and so was the white-washed room. There was a chair, a washstand and a chest of drawers. Baths took place by arrangement and were occasionally disappointing as regarded hot water.

It would, she supposed, be nice to say that you had been to Delphi, and Mrs. Peters had tried hard to take an interest in Ancient Greece, but she found it difficult. Their statuary seemed so unfinished; so lacking in heads and arms and legs. Secretly, she much preferred the handsome marble angel complete with wings which was erected on the late Mr. Willard Peters' tomb.

But all these secret opinions she kept carefully to herself, for fear her son Willard should despise her. It was for Willard's sake that she was here, in this chilly and uncomfortable room, with a sulky maid and a disgusted chauffeur in the offing.

For Willard (until recently called Junior—a title which he hated) was Mrs. Peters' eighteen-year-old son, and she worshipped him to distraction. It was Willard who had this strange passion for bygone art. It was Willard, thin, pale, spectacled and dyspeptic, who had dragged his adoring mother on this tour through Greece.

They had been to Olympia, which Mrs. Peters thought a sad mess. She had enjoyed the Parthenon, but she considered Athens a hopeless city. And a visit to Corinth and Mycenæ had been agony to both her and the chauffeur.

Delphi, Mrs. Peters thought unhappily, was the last straw. Absolutely nothing to do but walk along the road and look at the ruins. Willard spent long hours on his knees deciphering Greek inscriptions, saying, "Mother, just listen to this! Isn't it splendid?" And he would then read out something that seemed to Mrs. Peters the quintessence of dullness.

This morning Willard had started early to see some Byzantine mosaics. Mrs. Peters, feeling instinctively that Byzantine mosaics would leave her cold (in the literal as well as the spiritual sense), had excused herself.

"I understand, Mother," Willard had said. "You want to be alone just to sit in the theatre or up in the stadium and look down over it all and let it sink in."

"That's right, pet," said Mrs. Peters.

"I knew this place would get you," said Willard exultantly, and departed.

Now, with a sigh, Mrs. Peters prepared to rise and breakfast.

She came into the dining-room to find it empty save for four people. A mother and daughter, dressed in what seemed to Mrs. Peters a most peculiar style (not recognising the peplum as such), who were discoursing on the art of self-expression in dancing; a plump, middle-aged gentleman who had rescued a suit-case for her when she got off the train and whose name was Thompson; and a newcomer, a middle-aged gentleman with a bald head who had arrived on the preceding evening.

This personage was the last left in the breakfast room, and Mrs. Peters soon fell into conversation with him. She was a friendly woman and liked someone to talk to. Mr. Thompson had been distinctly discouraging in manner (British reserve, Mrs. Peters called it), and the mother and daughter had been very superior and highbrow, though the girl had got on rather well with Willard.

Mrs. Peters found the newcomer a very pleasant person. He was informative without being highbrow. He told her several interesting, friendly little details about the Greeks, which made her feel much more as though they were real people and not just tiresome history out of a book.

Mrs. Peters told her new friend all about Willard and what a clever boy he was, and how Culture might be said to be his middle name. There was something about this benevolent and bland personage which made him easy to talk to.

What he himself did and what his name was, Mrs. Peters did not learn. Beyond the fact that he had been travelling and that he was having a complete rest from business (what business?) he was not communicative about himself.

Altogether, the day passed more quickly than might have been anticipated. The mother and daughter and Mr. Thompson continued to be unsociable. They encountered the latter coming out of the museum, and he immediately turned in the opposite direction.

Mrs. Peters' new friend looked after him with a little frown.

"Now, I wonder who that fellow is!" he said.

Mrs. Peters supplied him with the other's name, but could do no more.

"Thompson—Thompson. No, I don't think I've met him before, and yet somehow or other his face seems familiar. But I can't place him."

In the afternoon Mrs. Peters enjoyed a quiet nap in a shady spot. The book she took with her to read was not the excellent one on Grecian Art recommended to her by her son, but was, on the contrary, entitled *The River Launch Mystery*. It had four murders in it, three abductions, and a large and varied gang of dangerous criminals. Mrs. Peters found herself both invigorated and soothed by the perusal of it.

It was four o'clock when she returned to the hotel. Willard, she felt sure, would be back by this time. So far was she from any presentiment of evil that she almost forgot to open a note which the proprietor said had been left for her by a strange man during the afternoon.

It was an extremely dirty note. Idly she ripped it open. As she read the first few lines, her face blanched and she put out a hand to steady herself. The handwriting was foreign but the language employed was English.

> Lady (it began),—This to hand to inform you that your son is being held captive by us in place of great security. No harm shall happen to honoured young gentleman if you obey orders of yours truly. We demand for him ransom of ten thousand English pounds sterling. If you speak of this to hotel proprietor or police or any such person your son will be killed. This is given you to reflect. To-morrow directions in way of paying money will be given. If not obeyed the honoured young gentleman's ears will be cut off and sent you. And following day if still not obeyed he will be killed. Again this is not idle threat. Let the Kyria reflect again—above all—be silent.
>
> Demetrius the Black Browed

It were idle to describe the poor lady's state of mind. Preposterous and childishly worded as the demand was, it yet brought home to her a grim atmosphere of peril. Willard, her boy, her pet, her delicate, serious Willard.

She would go at once to the police; she would rouse the neighbourhood. But perhaps, if she did—— She shivered.

Then, rousing herself, she went out of her room in search of the hotel proprietor—the sole person in the hotel who could speak English.

"It is getting late," she said. "My son has not returned yet."

The pleasant little man beamed at her. "True. Monsieur dismissed the mules. He wished to return on foot. He should have been here by now, but doubtless he has lingered on the way." He smiled happily.

"Tell me," said Mrs. Peters abruptly, "have you any bad characters in the neighbourhood?"

Bad characters was a term not embraced by the little man's knowledge of English. Mrs. Peters made her meaning plainer. She received in reply an assurance that all around Delphi were very good, very quiet people—all well disposed towards foreigners.

Words trembled on her lips, but she forced them back. That sinister threat tied her tongue. It might be the merest bluff. But suppose it wasn't? A friend of hers in America had had a child kidnapped, and on her informing the police, the child had been killed. Such things did happen.

She was nearly frantic. What was she to do? Ten thousand pounds—what was that?—between forty or fifty thousand dollars! What was that to her in comparison with Willard's safety? But how could she obtain such a sum? There were endless difficulties just now as regarded money and the drawing of cash. A letter of credit for a few hundred pounds was all she had with her.

Would the bandits understand this? Would they be reasonable? Would they *wait*?

When her maid came to her, she dismissed the girl fiercely. A bell sounded for dinner, and the poor lady was driven to the dining-room. She ate mechanically. She saw no one. The room might have been empty as far as she was concerned.

With the arrival of fruit, a note was placed before her. She winced, but the handwriting was entirely different from that which she had feared to see—a neat, clerkly English hand. She opened it without much interest, but she found its contents intriguing:

At Delphi you can no longer consult the Oracle (so it ran), but you *can* consult Mr. Parker Pyne.

Below that was a cutting of an advertisement pinned to the paper, and at the bottom of the sheet a passport photograph was attached. It was the photograph of her bald-headed friend of the morning.

Mrs. Peters read the printed cutting twice.

Are you happy? If not, consult Mr. Parker Pyne.

Happy? Happy? Had anyone ever been so *un*happy? It was like an answer to prayer.

Hastily she scribbled on a loose sheet of paper she happened to have in her bag:

Please help me. Will you meet me outside the hotel in ten minutes?

She enclosed it in an envelope and directed the waiter to take it to the gentleman at the table by the window. Ten minutes later, enveloped in a fur coat, for the night was chilly, Mrs. Peters went out of the hotel and strolled slowly along the road to the ruins. Mr. Parker Pyne was waiting for her.

"It's just the mercy of heaven you're here," said Mrs. Peters breathlessly. "But how did you guess the terrible trouble I'm in? That's what I want to know."

"The human countenance, my dear madam," said Mr. Parker Pyne gently. "I knew at once that *something* had happened, but what it is I am waiting for you to tell me."

Out it came in a flood. She handed him the letter, which he read by the light of his pocket torch.

"H'm," he said. "A remarkable document. A most remarkable document. It has certain points——"

But Mrs. Peters was in no mood to listen to a discussion of the finer points of the letter. What was she to do about Willard? Her own dear, delicate Willard.

Mr. Parker Pyne was soothing. He painted an attractive picture of Greek bandit life. They would be especially careful of their captive, since he represented a potential gold mine. Gradually he calmed her down.

"But what am I to *do*?" wailed Mrs. Peters.

"Wait till to-morrow," said Mr. Parker Pyne. "That is, unless you prefer to go straight to the police."

Mrs. Peters interrupted him with a shriek of terror. Her darling Willard would be murdered out of hand!

"You think I'll get Willard back safe and sound?"

"There is no doubt of that," said Mr. Parker Pyne soothingly. "The only question is whether you can get him back without paying ten thousand pounds."

"All I want is my boy."

"Yes, yes," said Mr. Parker Pyne soothingly. "Who brought the letter, by the way?"

"A man the landlord didn't know. A stranger."

"Ah! There are possibilities there. The man who brings the letter to-morrow might be followed. What are you telling the people at the hotel about your son's absence?"

"I haven't thought."

"I wonder, now." Mr. Parker Pyne reflected. "I think you might quite naturally express alarm and concern at his absence. A search party could be sent out."

"You don't think these fiends——?" She choked.

"No, no. So long as there is no word of the kidnapping or the ransom, they cannot turn nasty. After all, you can't be expected to take your son's disappearance with no fuss at all."

"Can I leave it all to you?"

"That is my business," said Mr. Parker Pyne.

They started back towards the hotel again but almost ran into a burly figure.

"Who was that?" asked Mr. Parker Pyne sharply.

"I think it was Mr. Thompson."

"Oh!" said Mr. Parker Pyne thoughtfully.

"Thompson, was it? Thompson—h'm."

Mrs. Peters felt as she went to bed that Mr. Parker Pyne's idea about the letter was a good one. Whoever brought it *must* be in touch with the bandits. She felt consoled, and fell asleep much sooner than she could ever have believed possible.

When she was dressing on the following morning she suddenly noticed something lying on the floor by the window. She picked it up—and her heart missed a beat. The same dirty, cheap envelope; the same hated characters. She tore it open.

Good-morning, lady. Have you made reflections? Your son is well and unharmed—so far. But we must have the money. It may not be easy for you to get this sum, but it has been told us that you have with you a necklace of diamonds. Very fine stones. We will be satisfied with that, instead. Listen, this is what you must do. You, or anyone you choose to send must take this necklace and bring it to the Stadium. From there go up to where there is a tree by a big rock. Eyes will watch and see that only one person comes. Then your son will be exchanged for necklace. The time must be to-morrow six o'clock in morning just after sunrise. If you put police on us afterwards we shoot your son as your car drives to station.

This is our last word, lady. If no necklace to-morrow morning your son's ears sent you. Next day he die.

With salutations, lady,

Demetrius

Mrs. Peters hurried to find Mr. Parker Pyne. He read the letter attentively.

"Is this true," he asked, "about a diamond necklace?"

"Absolutely. A hundred thousand dollars my husband paid for it."

"Our well-informed thieves," murmured Mr. Parker Pyne.

"What's that you say?"

"I was just considering certain aspects of the affair."

"My word, Mr. Pyne, we haven't got time for aspects. I've got to get my boy back."

"But you are a woman of spirit, Mrs. Peters. Do you enjoy being bullied and cheated out of ten thousand dollars? Do you enjoy giving up your diamonds meekly to a set of ruffians?"

"Well, of course, if you put it like that!" The woman of spirit in Mrs. Peters wrestled with the mother. "How I'd like to get even with them—the cowardly brutes! The very minute I get my boy back, Mr. Pyne, I shall set the whole police of the neighbourhood on them, and, if necessary, I shall hire an armoured car to take Willard and myself to the railway station!" Mrs. Peters was flushed and vindictive.

"Ye-es," said Mr. Parker Pyne. "You see, my dear madam, I'm afraid they will be prepared for that move on your part. They know that once Willard is restored to you nothing will keep you from setting the whole neighbourhood on the alert. Which leads one to suppose that they have prepared for that move."

"Well, what do you want to do?"

Mr. Parker Pyne smiled. "I want to try a little plan of my own." He looked round the dining-room. It was empty and the doors at both ends were closed. "Mrs. Peters, there is a man I know in Athens—a jeweller. He specialises in good artificial diamonds—first-class stuff." His voice dropped to a whisper. "I'll get him by telephone. He can get here this afternoon, bringing a good selection of stones with him."

"You mean?"

"He'll extract the real diamonds and replace them with paste replicas."

"Why, if that isn't the cutest thing I've ever heard of!" Mrs. Peters gazed at him with admiration.

"Sh! Not so loud. Will you do something for me?"

"Surely."

"See that nobody comes within earshot of the telephone."

Mrs. Peters nodded.

The telephone was in the manager's office. He vacated it obligingly, after having helped Mr. Parker Pyne to obtain the number. When he emerged, he found Mrs. Peters outside.

"I'm just waiting for Mr. Parker Pyne," she said. "We're going for a walk."

"Oh, yes, madam."

Mr. Thompson was also in the hall. He came towards them and engaged the manager in conversation.

Were there any villas to be let in Delphi? No? But surely there was one above the hotel.

"That belongs to a Greek gentleman, monsieur. He does not let it."

"And there are no other villas?"

"There is one belonging to an American lady. That is the other side of the village. It is shut up now. And there is one belonging to an English gentleman, an artist—that is on the cliff edge looking down to Itéa."

Mrs. Peters broke in. Nature had given her a loud voice and she purposely made it louder. "Why," she said, "I'd just adore to have a villa here! So unspoilt and natural. I'm simply crazy about the place, aren't you, Mr. Thompson? But of course you must be if you want a villa. Is it your first visit here? You don't say so."

She ran on determinedly till Mr. Parker Pyne emerged

from the office. He gave her just the faintest smile of approval.

Mr. Thompson walked slowly down the steps and out into the road, where he joined the highbrow mother and daughter, who seemed to be feeling the wind cold on their exposed arms.

All went well. The jeweller arrived just before dinner with a car full of other tourists. Mrs. Peters took her necklace to his room. He grunted approval. Then he spoke in French.

"*Madame peut être tranquille. Je reussirai.*" He extracted some tools from his little bag and began work.

At eleven o'clock Mr. Parker Pyne tapped on Mrs. Peters' door. "Here you are!"

He handed her a little chamois bag. She glanced inside.

"My diamonds!"

"Hush. Here is the necklace with the paste replacing the diamonds. Pretty good, don't you think?"

"Simply wonderful."

"Aristopoulos is a clever fellow."

"You don't think they'll suspect?"

"How should they? They know you have the necklace with you. You hand it over. How can they suspect the trick?"

"Well, I think it's wonderful," Mrs. Peters reiterated, handing the necklace back to him. "Will you take it to them? Or is that asking too much of you?"

"Certainly I will take it. Just give me the letter, so that I have the directions clear. Thank you. Now, good-night and *bon courage*. Your boy will be with you to-morrow for breakfast."

"Oh, if only that's true!"

"Now, don't worry. Leave everything in my hands."

Mrs. Peters did not spend a good night. When she slept, she had terrible dreams. Dreams where armed bandits in armoured cars fired off a fusillade at Williard, who was running down the mountain in his pyjamas.

She was thankful to wake. At last came the first glimmer of dawn. Mrs. Peters got up and dressed. She sat—waiting.

At seven o'clock there came a tap on her door. Her throat was so dry she could hardly speak.

"Come in," she said.

The door opened and Mr. Thompson entered. She stared at him. Words failed her. She had a sinister presentiment of disaster. And yet his voice when he spoke was completely natural and matter-of-fact. It was a rich, bland voice.

"Good-morning, Mrs. Peters," he said.

"How dare you, sir! How dare you——"

"You must excuse my unconventional visit at so early an hour," said Mr. Thompson. "But you see, I have a matter of business to transact."

Mrs. Peters leaned forward with accusing eyes. "So it was you who kidnapped my boy! It wasn't bandits at all!"

"It certainly wasn't bandits. Most unconvincingly done, that part of it, I thought. Inartistic, to say the least of it."

Mrs. Peters was a woman of a single idea. "Where's my boy?" she demanded, with the eyes of an angry tigress.

"As a matter of fact," said Mr. Thompson, "he's just outside the door."

"Willard!"

The door was flung open. Willard, sallow and spectacled and distinctly unshaven, was clasped to his mother's heart. Mr. Thompson stood looking benignly on.

"All the same," said Mrs. Peters, suddenly recovering herself and turning on him, "I'll have the law on you for this. Yes, I will."

"You've got it all wrong, Mother," said Willard. "This gentleman rescued me."

"Where were you?"

"In a house on the cliff point. Just a mile from here."

"And allow me, Mrs. Peters," said Mr. Thompson, "to restore your property."

He handed her a small packet loosely wrapped in tissue paper. The paper fell away and revealed the diamond necklace.

"You need not treasure that other little bag of stones, Mrs. Peters," said Mr. Thompson, smiling. "The real stones are still in the necklace. The chamois bag contains some excellent imitation stones. As your friend said, Aristopoulos is quite a genius."

"I just don't understand a word of all this," said Mrs. Peters faintly.

"You must look at the case from my point of view," said

Mr. Thompson. "My attention was caught by the use of a certain name. I took the liberty of following you and your fat friend out of doors and I listened—I admit it frankly—to your exceedingly interesting conversation. I found it remarkably suggestive, so much so that I took the manager into my confidence. He took a note of the number to which your plausible friend telephoned and he also arranged that a waiter should listen to your conversation in the dining-room this morning.

"The whole scheme worked out very clearly. You were being made the victim of a couple of clever jewel thieves. They know all about your diamond necklace; they follow you here; they kidnap your son, and write the rather comic 'bandit' letter, and they arrange that you shall confide in the chief instigator of the plot.

"After that, all is simple. The good gentleman hands you a bag of imitation diamonds and—clears out with his pal. This morning, when your son did not appear, you would be frantic. The absence of your friend would lead you to believe that he had been kidnapped, too. I gather that they had arranged for someone to go to the villa to-morrow. That person would have discovered your son, and by the time you and he had put your heads together you might have got an inkling of the plot. But by that time the villains would have got an excellent start."

"And now?"

"Oh, now they are safely under lock and key. I arranged for that."

"The villain," said Mrs. Peters, wrathfully remembering her own trustful confidences. "The oily, plausible villain."

"Not at all a nice fellow," agreed Mr. Thompson.

"It beats me how you got on to it," said Willard admiringly. "Pretty smart of you."

The other shook his head deprecatingly. "No, no," he said. "When you are travelling incognito and hear your own name being taken in vain——"

Mrs. Peters stared at him. "Who are you?" she demanded abruptly.

"*I am Mr. Parker Pyne,*" explained that gentleman.

THE END